Joe Harris,
The Moon

Joyce A. Miller

Joyce A. Miller
www.joyceamiller.com

Joe Harris The Moon is a work of fiction. My imagined Joe Harris, his wife Pearl and other well-known historical figures in the story do abide by the generally known facts of the real Harris's life. I have sometimes quoted real newspaper articles and radio broadcasts. Other names, characters, places and events are products of my imagination and any resemblance to actual persons, living or dead, events or locales is entirely coincidental.

Book Layout © 2020 BookDesignTemplates.com
Book Cover © 2020 Oliver J. Dimalanta

Joe Harris, the Moon/ Joyce A. Miller. -- 1st ed.
ISBN 978-1-7354963-0-6 Paperback
ISBN 978-1-7354963-1-3 E-Book

Dedicated to my cousin Bob(by)

CONTENTS

CHAPTER ONE

1903

Joe's eyes popped open in the early morning darkness knowing this was the day he would join the other men in his family in the coal mines. He knew mining for the rest of his life wasn't for him, unlike his father and brothers. He silently pledged to himself, "I will be a baseball player. What can I do today to make that happen?"

It wasn't long before Joe heard his mother's call from downstairs. "Boys! It's time to get up."

William, James, Thomas, and Joe slowly rustled from under the faded quilts that had a film of black dust on them. Joe shared a bedroom with three of his brothers and shared a bed with one. The bedsteads were iron with feather mattresses. Joe liked to stretch his arms over his head, sink down into the soft mattress and then grasp the iron bar at the head of the bed before he threw the covers off and jumped out. His bedmate, six-year-old Thomas, would yell out when the chilly air hit him. It was still a little dark outside, and his brothers enjoyed catching a few more moments of sleep rather than being the first to head outside to the privy.

Joe put his ear to the wall to see if he could hear his older brothers, Enoch, Jack, and David stirring in the bedroom next door. He moved to the second story window, pulled back the dusty curtain and looked down at the yard below. He could see the row of outhouses behind each of the houses on the street. At least it wasn't raining. He went first, racing out of the bedroom and down the stairs barefoot, still wearing his long underwear.

He met back up with his brothers and the rest of the family at the breakfast table. His mother ladled up big portions of oatmeal with sweet prunes for them to eat. They washed it all down with cups of coffee. With six brothers and two sisters living in the house together, there wasn't always an abundance to eat, but Joe's mother, Annie, tried her best to feed them all. Each man who worked in the mine made $10 a week for six full days. James, who was only three years older than Joe, made a little less because he worked with the animals. Out of their pay, they had to pay the mining company back for their coveralls and boots, safety lamps, rent, and coal for heat. Annie insisted that they tithe to the church. Groceries were the last item on the list, and even with all the boys pitching in the staples didn't stretch far. Joe's dad, Joseph Sr., had been a coal miner in Staffordshire, England, and emigrated to this part of Pennsylvania over 30 years ago and continued coal mining. Annie was from Lanarkshire, Scotland. She met Joseph on the boat and married him when they settled in Coulters, Pennsylvania.

Now that it was May and the end of the school year, Joe had finished with the eighth grade and would no longer attend school. It was time for him to join his dad and his older brothers Enoch, Jack, David, William, and James at the coal mine. Although William was only sixteen, he was big for his age and moved up to become a coal miner. Joe would take his place with James tending to the donkeys. Tending the animals was one of the jobs given to twelve-year-old boys at the mine. Only one of Joe's older brothers escaped the mine by working at a farm.

"Eat up, Joe. And quit staring at the baseball scores in yesterday's paper," Enoch said as he tousled Joe's hair. "Don't want to be late for your first day." Joe looked up to Enoch, his oldest brother, because he was always helping his parents with the family. Twenty years older than Joe, Enoch had never married and still lived at home with them as most immigrant miners did. He was taller than Joe by at least 6 inches. When he slipped on his miner's hat, only a small shock of his mousey brown hair showed over his kind blue eyes and pale freckled face. Joe and all of his brothers resembled their father with those same facial features and coloring.

Joe scoured the paper every day for baseball news. He was a loyal fan of the Pittsburgh Pirates and expected them to win every game they played. With Pittsburgh only twenty miles from Coulters, the Pirates were his hometown team. Usually at this time in May when school ended he would head for the baseball fields to play with his friends every day the sun shined. Baseball was one bright light in a dreary existence for all the miners and their children.

Enoch and Joe grabbed the metal pails their mother had packed for them and headed out the door behind the others. Like a school of fish, Joseph Sr. and his six sons joined the wave of other men who were leaving their houses and walking towards the mine. They quietly marched down the grimy street past straight rows of houses, all painted the same dull red color. All the houses were coated in black dust. Joe occasionally looked up at the blue Allegheny Mountains jutting up behind them in the sunrise.

At the end of the street they came to the mine entrance. This was where Enoch and the other men were swallowed whole by the dark, cavernous mouth of the mine. Huge wooden oak beams surrounded the gloomy entrance. A heavy wooden door rode on overhead rails, and the door boys opened and closed it as each car passed in and out. Small chunks of rock were scattered on the dirt floor that had been tamped down by thousands of miners crossing the threshold. The miners all knew this was a dangerous, dismal place. Many of those who worked below the ground knew the dangers that might threaten their lives. If they weren't crushed by rock or burned by exploding gas lines, then they could certainly expect to get miner's asthma from breathing the bad air.

James and Joe carried on down the road where the barnyard scent of manure, hay, and wet animals hit them before they saw the actual stable. Although William was moving up, James was only 15 years old, and he continued working in the stable. They met up with the stableman, Mr. Campbell, at the entrance. Mr. Campbell had tufts of grey hair sticking out behind his ears. One of the straps of his denim overalls slid a few inches off his stooped shoulders. He had the sleeves of his flannel shirt rolled up to his elbows. He chewed on a piece of straw he held in the side of his mouth.

"Mr. Campbell? This here's my brother, Joe. He'll be taking William's place working with me here in the stables. William has moved on to work the seams." James said to the older man stooped over a barrel of grain.

"Do you know anythin' about donkeys or mules, young Joe?" Mr. Campbell asked as he limped from the barrel of grain to the entrance of the stables.

"I just know what my brothers have told me. I'm a quick learner, sir. And I like animals," Joe replied. James winked his approval at Joe as he moved on to take care of his own animal.

"You're goin' to be takin' care of George here. We keep three donkeys goin' at all times. They ain't like horses, and the rain will seep right into his coat so you have to keep him dry. He needs water every day and he don't like it dirty. That will be no easy feat for you seein's as how it's always dirty here near the mine. He'll be outside grazin' all night, but he'll still need some food scraps now and again. You're to wash his food bucket every day. That's enough for now. We'll talk about feet and teeth tomorrow. So, you go fill his food bucket and then clean it out. Then we'll tack him up to the cart. Unnerstand?" Mr. Campbell asked.

"Yes, sir." Joe said.

Joe took George by the halter and led him from his stall into the aisle way of the barn. Slivers of sunlight shined on the black coal dust that coated the barn.

"Aw-ee-aw," George sounded. He already wanted his food. Joe fed him some scraps from the bucket, and then he brushed some coal dust out of his grey coat. He had to hook George up to the cart. Joe wasn't sure how he would put all those pieces of the driving gear together. James had explained the procedure to him. So many buckles! The piece he looked for first was the breast halter. Then he found the little saddle and girth straps. And finally, he grabbed the breeching piece. The crouper went around George's tail, and the breeching piece went around George's rump. After those pieces were in place, he tightened the girth. Joe could tell that George was holding his breath so that the girth wouldn't be too tight.

"You're a tricky one, George," Joe said. "But I'm a step ahead of you." Joe walked George around in a small circle until he was breathing again. Then Joe tightened the girth.

Joe continued thinking to himself about the things that James told him: "The saddle holds the shafts of the cart. The breeching is the brakes. The traces pull the cart. The shafts just hold the cart up. When your donkey leans on the breast halter, the cart will go forward." Joe wasn't giving up, and he wanted to show Mr. Campbell that he didn't need help on his first day in the stable. The last piece to go on was the driving bridle with blinkers. Joe was very careful with George's long ears as he put the bridle on him. The blinkers would keep George from looking all around him. Once the blinkers were on, Joe kept touching George since he couldn't see him when he was behind him. He didn't want George to kick him and give him a limp like Mr. Campbell had.

Then Joe hitched George to the cart. First, he did one side and then the other. He wanted the straps snug but not too tight. He went back and checked everything twice on the cart. He didn't want to have the donkey halfway down the mine shaft and have a buckle come loose. Then Joe took up the reins.

"Walk on," Joe said to George. He stood far enough behind so that George couldn't kick him. Joe was patient. Slowly the cart went forward. The wooden cart seemed heavy even though there was no load in it yet. He walked with George into a line behind the other boys with their donkeys. James was ahead of him. Mr. Campbell gave Joe a nod as he left the stable. They all made their way to the mine entrance.

Because these were underground mines, the donkeys walked with the carts partially down into the mine shafts. Sometimes George would slip, and Joe would have to reassure him to get him going again. The boys and donkeys backed the cart up to the pit, and the miner filled the cart with huge chunks of coal. When the cart was full, they took it back to the surface and other miners emptied it into a tub.

The first day wasn't so bad. Just back and forth. Back and forth. James met Joe back in the stable when the sun was beginning to set.

"Joe, you know to untack the donkey, you just do everything in reverse that you did this morning," James said. "And remember to pick his hooves before you put him out."

"Would you show me how to do that?" Joe asked.

James demonstrated with his donkey. "You stand next to him facing his tail. You run your hand down his leg and he'll pick up his foot. You support his foot against your knee. Then you take this metal hoof pick and clean out any pieces of coal, rocks or dirt from that fleshy triangle in the middle of his hoof. Then you slowly set his foot down. If you let him put his own foot down, he may squish one of your toes."

They untacked their donkeys, picked their hooves and put them out in the pasture. Then they mucked the manure out of their stalls and put down fresh straw for the next morning. The donkeys didn't live long with their tough miner lives, but because they made money for the mine owners they were as well managed as the mine owners could do. The owners insisted on so many quarts of grain and so much hay in the evening.

"I'll see you tomorrow, George," Joe said as he opened the pasture gate and patted George on the rump. George brayed and skittered into the field.

Joe and James didn't speak as they started the long walk home. Covered from head to toe in black dust, Joe was so tired he could barely put one foot in front of the other. They took their coveralls off on the porch before they went into the house. Then they went to the pump outside and washed off as much of the grime on their hands and faces as they could. They made their way back to the kitchen where their mother was getting dinner on the table.

"How was your first day?" Annie asked him as she ladled the stew made mostly of potatoes into his bowl. She was wearing a floor length calico dress with a white apron around her waist.

"It was OK, Mum. I'm just really tired." Joe replied. Joe held up his head by propping both elbows on the table. Both Enoch and William laughed. They knew how exhausted Joe would be from now on. But with eleven people at the dinner table all talking at once, Joe hardly heard them laughing.

After dinner they lit the gas lamp and sat in the living room. Enoch, Mary, Jack, David and William pulled out a deck of cards to play, but Joe was too tired. He went upstairs with his youngest brother, Thomas. Joe pulled back the dusty covers and went to bed.

"We missed you at school today, Joe," Thomas said into the darkness of the bedroom. "It doesn't seem the same there without you."

Joe didn't hear what he said because he was already fast asleep.

Their mother called upstairs again the next morning. But this day was a rainy one. Off they went to the stables to hitch up the donkeys in the rain and mud. Joe thought he was bone-tired the first day—but the second day proved even worse. Mud covered everything.

This lifestyle went on for months. Throughout the summer, Joe hitched George up to his cart. Filled and re-filled the cart with huge coal chunks. Emptied the cart. Then did the whole thing over again.

In the fall when the leaves were changing color, everything was prettier. The mountains of southwestern Pennsylvania were magical shades of gold, orange, and red in the fall. As tired as he was every day, when October rolled around Joe would race home from the stable, throwing leaves into the air and swinging at them with an imaginary bat. He wanted to see the headline in the newspaper with the baseball score for the day. The Pittsburgh Pirates were headed to the first ever World Series.

Joe's enthusiasm was short-lived. The Pirates started off well, but the Boston Americans ended up winning the series.

"When I'm older, I'm going to play for the Pittsburgh Pirates," Joe whispered in George's ear as he tacked him up the next day.

With winter the snow came down. George grew a winter coat, and Joe wore a heavy jacket, gloves, and boots. The boys attached snowplows to the donkeys' harnesses, and they cleared a path to the mine opening. But by the time the donkeys hauled up their first loads of coal, the wind blew drifts of snow back over the path. The snow stuck to George's fur and eyelashes. Small clouds of warm air puffed out of his nostrils.

Joe constantly reassured George in the snow. "Walk on, George. Good boy. Good job," he'd say over and over. He made clicking sounds with his mouth that George seemed to like.

"Whoa, boy," he'd say when they finally made it back to the stable. Joe picked the ice out of George's hooves, brushed as much dirt out of his coat as he could before he put a thick canvas blanket on him. He put him in a warm, straw-filled stall for the night. Joe headed for home himself, throwing a snowball up into the air and then catching it as if he was tagging someone out at first base.

Chapter Two

1904

When Valentine's Day came around, Joe had to admit he missed going to school. It was a bright spot in the grey days of winter. All the students in school made Valentine's Day cards with bits of colored paper glued to post-cards. Some of the students' families could afford printed valentines, but the Harris family couldn't. The students set up a faux post office. Two girls ran the post office, and the rest of the children got the mail. It took about an hour to distribute all of the cards, and the anticipation was part of the fun. The kids read the verses out loud to each other and laughed. The teacher usually brought candy for everyone. It was one of the few times during the year that the children got candy.

When seven-year-old Thomas got home from school and Joe got home from the mine, Thomas showed Joe the cards he received. "I got five. Two ugly ones and three pretty ones. The teacher, Mrs. Robinson, got nine. But I also got this one addressed to you."

Joe slowly opened the card. It was handdrawn with *Me + You* over a red heart with an arrow through it. Someone had written, "You is my best friend" with a scratchy black crayon. Nothing else.

"Who sent this?" Joe asked, his face turning red with embarrassment. Thomas shrugged.

"It just came from the school post office along with all the others. But it seems like someone likes you," Thomas teased in a singsong voice. He made kissing sounds with his mouth in Joe's direction.

Joe punched him in the arm. Thomas started to cry.

"Joseph, stop hitting your brother," Annie called from the kitchen. "You're a lot bigger than he is." She only called him by his full name when she was angry with him. "What is all the fuss about?" she asked as she rustled into the front room. Thomas sniffled as his nose ran from the tears.

"He was teasing me about this Valentine I got," Joe said. "I just wanted to know who sent it."

"Maybe you'll never know. That's no reason to hit your brother," Annie said. "Some girls like to keep these things to themselves. Just know that you have a secret admirer."

Annie shared a knowing glance with Thomas, and he stopped crying. When Joe saw that, he thought maybe the two of them had sent the valentine to him as a prank. He put the card away in his top dresser drawer anyway.

That evening at dinner, Annie served some canned pears for dessert. Although her hands were red and rough from all the housework she did, she gingerly ladled two pear halves onto each dish. One of her neighbors had preserved them and given them to Annie as a gift.

"What a treat," Joseph Sr. said.

"Well, it's Valentine's Day," Annie said. "Thomas and I have to 'fess up to something. We knew that Joe was missing school, and we thought we'd send him a little card. It was all in fun. But it turned out wrong, and we don't want Joe's feelings to be hurt."

"Thank you, Mum. To tell you the truth, I'm relieved," Joe said. "I didn't think I could handle having a girlfriend right now. I don't even remember the names of the girls at the school." Joe tried to enjoy his pears but couldn't help feeling the gritty coal dust in his teeth that went along with almost every bite he took.

His brothers grinned at him as they ate their dessert. They knew that Joe had a one-track mind and that one track was base-ball. Girls never entered his mind. He sometimes even slept with his baseball mitt.

"Don't hold it against your brother. It was my idea," Annie said as she began clearing the dishes from the table into the kitchen. Annie was a tough woman, but she had a soft spot in her heart for Joe. Joe's two sisters helped her scrub the plates, cutlery, and pots with the carbolic soap in the huge white enamel pan. Then they set everything to dry on the sideboard.

Before Joe went to bed, he glanced into the front parlor where he saw his mother working on a quilt. The quilt was a hodgepodge mix of colors and textures. She pulled from a pile of scraps of corduroy, wool, flannel, and cotton from some of their old clothes. Annie looked up from her sewing.

"Come and sit beside me while I do this piecework, Joe. This piece here is from your sister Margaret's dress that she wore first day to school. And this blue cotton shirt was one of David's favorites. I look at this quilt and I can see my children growing up. I raised ten children in this house. Of course, you're probably thinking, we're no different than anyone else in this town. Everyone has all of their children in the house,"

Annie said. Annie fingered the quilt absentmindedly as she talked.

Joe pointed at a piece of brown corduroy. "I remember those pants," he said.

"That's right. Those were your Sunday school pants. And then Thomas wore them after you. But the knees were so worn out that I decided it was time for them to go into the quilt."

"It's fetching, Mum," Joe said. "It paints a picture of our lives."

"Well, thank you, honey. When I first started sewing it up, I thought I might sell it. But now I think I'll keep it. Maybe replace the one that's on your bed. Would you like that?"

"I'd like that," Joe looked pleased. "And now I'll head up to bed and get under the warm quilt that's already up there."

Joe leaned over and gave his mother a kiss on the cheek. "Off with you, now," she said.

Winter turned to spring, and the warm weather was welcome. Joe liked to look up at the sun and feel its warmth on his face as he walked George back and forth to the mine entrance. He had grown quite fond of old George.

One evening in May, Joe's dad was sitting on the porch rocker after dinner reading the newspaper. Fireflies were beginning to glow in the small front yard. Joe was sitting on the porch steps throwing a baseball into the air and catching it in his glove. "Look at this headline, Joe," he said. "CY YOUNG DOES NOT LET ONE OF THE ATHLETICS REACH FIRST BASE."

Joe took the stairs two at a time and landed with a thud on the wooden porch. He hovered over his father's shoulder and read the beginning of the article aloud. "Athletics don't make a hit, and Cyrus doesn't give a base on balls. Then to make the job complete, the Bostonians play without a fielding error."

"I would love to be there in Boston," Joe said wistfully. "That Cy Young is something. A perfect game. Has anyone ever done that before? That would be so exciting to see. We should have tried to go to one of the World Series games last year. Then we could have seen him with our own eyes. Right here in Pittsburgh."

"You know we can't afford to do things like that, Joe. He sure is a great pitcher. He would have kept you busy at first base, wouldn't he?" Joseph said to his son with amusement touched with a little sadness.

"I would work with him for every put out," Joe said. He threw the ball in the air, caught it in his glove, and touched his dad on the leg as if he was tagging him on first base.

"I'm out!" Joseph clenched his right fist and lifted it up towards his head, making the umpire's sign for calling someone out at base.

Joe looked at the lined, deep furrows in his father's tired, face. Although they had these small moments of fun, his dad would soon be turning sixty and he still had to go to work at the mine every day. He would never retire. He had done the best he could for his family, but Joe wanted more. Joe had been bitten by the baseball bug and wanted to go to ball games. To play in ball games. To be outside in the sunshine every day.

Joe was used to working with his donkey and cart daily, and he was getting much stronger. He didn't get so tired now. At lunchtime, Joe would gather several other boys who were tending to the donkeys or handling the doors and they would squeeze in an inning or two of baseball. There were never enough boys to make complete teams on either side. Joe made a couple of balls by winding string around a rubber core and then covering it with tape. Joe started packing his baseball glove in with his lunch pail. He'd put a drop of neat oil on the glove and push a ball inside it before packing it. He loved the smell of leather along with the yeasty bread sandwiches when he opened his lunch pail. It sure beat the smell of the stable.

On the way home from the mine, Joe and his brothers would steal a few minutes to play catch and try to pick up ground balls. Even though Jack was almost 30 years old, he liked to play with Joe, William, and David. They passed a baseball field on their way to the mines every day. The field was not level and the ground balls would pop up, but the field was all they had so they used it. When the days got longer in the summer, they could return to the field after dinner and get a pickup game going.

Joe relied on strategy more than power because he was younger than the other players at only thirteen. He was great at stealing bases. So, Joe always got picked to be on a team.

One warm evening the boys were playing a game, and a crowd developed to watch them. Joe was up to bat and the bases were loaded. Joe closed his eyes for a moment. He blocked out the hubbub of the crowd and the opposing team's chatter. The pitcher spit on the ball, and it made a wavy, crazy way to home plate.

Crack! Joe made contact with the soft ball despite its loopy path to get to him. The ball sailed over the center fielder's head, and Joe easily loped around the bases. Joe's team won the game 7 to 2. All the guys swarmed around him, patting him on the back.

"Great game, Joe," his brother Jack said. "You put it all out there on that field."

"You have such great instinct for hitting," William said, with his arms folded in front of him.

Joe smiled from ear to ear as the small crowd clapped and shouted congratulations. For a moment Joe felt young and carefree like the teenager he was. His heart felt light when he was playing baseball well. Like a sponge absorbing water, Joe soaked up his older brothers' admiration.

But the next morning, Joe's good mood disappeared when he was back in the stable getting George out of the stall and harnessing him to the cart. The whole time he was down in the dark mineshaft waiting for his next load of coal, trudging through the dirty seam water in the ditches on the way to the surface, he was thinking about that baseball game. He could almost smell the grass and the fresh air. He loved the game.

Chapter Three

1908

Joe had been working in the mine for five years. Every day seemed the same. In the winter he was always cold, and in the summer he was always hot. Everything always covered in dust. The only pleasure he got was playing pickup baseball with his brothers and a few of their friends.

In January, Joe's family read the news of the Darr Mine disaster in Jacob's Creek, only 20 miles away. There was an explosion in the mine, and over 300 men and boys were killed. It was the same type of mine where the Harris family men worked. The explosion was most likely caused by an open flame lamp in an area where there were high levels of gas and coal dust. Joe was horrified by the images and stories in the paper. Many of the charred bodies were of the trapper boys, boys who were Joe's age who had the job of opening and closing the trap doors to let the mining cars through. Due to the lack of ventilation underground, these boys spent most days sitting in darkness and swiftly opening the doors for the mine carts. At least Joe got to go outside of the mine shafts when he walked George's cart out.

Annie wept when she read the story of the German woman who lost her husband and both of her boys, her only children. Many workers took their children into the mine to help with the work. The woman's youngest son was only 16 years old. And her other son, also named Joe, wouldn't have been in the mine that day except that he took the place of a sick neighbor. He was happy to get a couple of days' wages as a machine worker. Now he lay blackened and disfigured with the other corpses at the entrance to the mine, and he was only 19 years old. The images in the newspaper of the women and children huddled at the mine's entrance awaiting word on whether their loved ones were dead or alive were haunting.

Joe was seventeen years old now. No longer the scrawny twelve-year-old who harnessed his donkey for his trips back and forth to the mine entrance each day. Joe never got as tall as his brothers; he seemed to have stopped growing at 5 foot 9 inches. He was stocky with thick legs, and his brothers were lanky. He had the same coffee-colored hair, blue-gray eyes, and pale freckled skin of all the Harris men. Although he wasn't sad, his mouth turned slightly downwards at both sides, making him look like he was frowning. He didn't smile very much. His eyes turned downwards at the sides, too, to match his mouth. His round ears stuck out from the sides of his head, making a seat for his ever-present baseball cap.

"Joe, head over to McKeesport and see if they'll let you play on their team," old Mr. Campbell told him one day in the spring. "The mine, here, doesn't have a team—but McKeesport Tube Works has a team that would probably love to have you. I've watched you play after work."

"What do you mean, the company has a baseball team?" Joe asked.

"The McKeesport Tube Works is a steel mill that makes pipe and tube. And they have a baseball team. If you get picked to be on the baseball team, they'll also give you a job at the mill. And you can get out of this mine. Not sayin' that the mill would be a whole lot safer. They have just as many accidents in the mills. But you'd be above ground. You should go," Mr. Campbell replied.

"Thanks, Mr. Campbell, for lookin' out for me. I'm gonna do that. Next chance I get," Joe said.

Joe could hardly believe this. And McKeesport was only nine miles away. He could have been playing baseball all this time instead of walking George back and forth up the mine road?

On one of his few days off, Joe headed down Long Run Road with his glove tucked under his arm. He left before dark because he knew it would take him about three hours to walk to McKeesport. He walked along the Youghiogheny River near the railroad tracks. The river water was rushing quickly over boulders and tree trunks. The water level was higher than normal due to the spring rains. Joe closed his eyes and listened to the sound of the rushing water. He could hear a bird call out now and then. Cicadas were humming. Most of the walk from Coulters around the big bend of the Youghiogheny was rural, but as he approached McKeesport he saw a few more houses. He smelled some freshly mown grass. He heard a few wind chimes twinkling on porches. He whistled while he walked.

He came to the ball field on the edge of the big steel mill. As he got closer, the sky got darker and heavier with smoke. Orange flames were spewing into the air, even in the middle of the day. The air smelled of sulfur like rotten eggs. Joe stood next to the fence on the Tubers' side of the field as the teams were warming up. Two players were throwing a ball back and forth.

A grizzled old man walked up to where Joe was standing and spat into the dirt. The gray stubble on his wrinkled face matched the short gray hair on his head. He noticed Joe had his baseball mitt tucked under his arm.

"Play ball?" he asked.

Joe nodded his head. "I play with my brothers and a few friends, every chance I get."

"Where?" the old man asked.

"In Coulters. At the mine," Joe replied.

"What position?" the man asked.

"First base. Or outfield," Joe told him.

"I've heard about a young kid, playing first base at the mine," the curmudgeon said. "You're also pretty good with the stick."

That surprised Joe. Had Mr. Campbell talked to this man? The man was wearing a team jacket and cap, but he seemed too old to be a part of the team.

"Name is Cutter. I'm the manager here," Cutter said.

Joe stammered and shook his hand. He hoped his hand wasn't sweaty. "P-p-pleased to meet you, Mr. Cutter. I'm Joe Harris."

"Harris. Harris. There are more Harris' than just you? That name sounds familiar." Cutter said in a brittle voice that sounded like it would break at any moment.

"I have two other brothers who play," Joe said.

"Harris, we're short a man today. Would you like to step in and play for him?" Cutter asked.

"Yes, sir! I would!"

Cutter yelled to someone in the dugout. "Take young Joe here in the clubhouse and get him a uniform. Then bring him back out here."

Joe followed the other player into the clubhouse and put on a uniform that was a little too big for his 5' 9" frame. The white wool uniform was heavy and hot—but Joe didn't care because this was his chance to play baseball with a team. He buttoned the front of the shirt and tucked it into his pants. The shirt had "Tubers" in blue embroidered letters across the front. The best part of the uniform was the colored stockings. Joe sat on the bench and kept holding up each leg in front of himself to look at them. First one leg and then the other. Because he lived in faded hand-me-downs from his brothers, he had never owned a piece of clothing that was such a bright blue color as those stockings.

He ran out of the clubhouse and into the dugout with the rest of the Tubers. They had already dressed and were ready to play ball.

Cutter introduced him to the other players. "This here's Joe Harris. He'll be playing in right field for us—just for today."

Joe smiled and got a few hellos and welcomes from the other players. He looked up into the bleachers and noticed there were dozens of fans ready to watch the game.

Everything was going fine until the bottom of the fourth inning when things unraveled. Joe didn't communicate with the center fielder, and it caused the ball to bounce into the bullpen for a ground-rule double. The pitcher was slow to cover first base on a slow hopper to the first baseman. The base runner was called safe, and a run scored. And it continued on like this with this switch in the momentum until the Tubers had lost the game. 12 to 2. Joe hung his head as he walked off the field.

"That's just one game, guys," Cutter told the players in the clubhouse. "Just one game. We'll be back tomorrow." But he nodded toward Joe and took him aside from the other guys. "I'm sorry, Harris, but you're just not ready yet. Practice a little more with your friends and come back in a year or two."

Joe stared at the coal dust under his fingernails as he unbuttoned his uniform and put back on his grungy mine clothes. Joe rolled up the blue stockings and stuck them in his pants pocket. He couldn't bear to part with them. On the way home, the nine mile walk back along the river was not pleasant. It was dusk, and he kicked his feet in the dust on the side of the road as he walked. He replayed the game repeatedly in his head.

When he got home, Enoch was waiting for him in the kitchen. "How did it go?" he quietly asked his little brother, although he could guess from Joe's down expression.

Joe felt ashamed as he mumbled, "It couldn't get any worse. I made some mistakes. They told me to come back in a year or two. I just wanted to be part of a team, like being part of this family, but bigger, you know?"

"I saved you a little bit of this salad from dinner. I thought you might be hungry after your long day. The girls went and picked some dandelion greens. Mum made salad from them with a dressing of bacon grease and vinegar, and hard-boiled eggs."

"Thanks, Enoch. But I'm really not hungry," Joe said. When Enoch produced the salad from under the towel that was covering it, Joe's mouth started to water. "Well, maybe I'll eat a little bit of it. I wouldn't want to hurt Mum's feelings."

Enoch knew what it was like to spend years in the mine. He thought about the recent mine explosion and how the difference between life and death was the speed with which the rescuers got to the miners. If the men weren't killed in the initial explosion, then the deadly fumes would kill them before they got to the surface for fresh air. He didn't want that future for his brother. He said, "There'll be other chances for you, little brother. You're good at baseball. Don't give up."

The next morning, Joe walked back up the dusty road to the mine with his brothers and the other men. George, who was braying loudly, waited for him. Joe felt down and out about his life even as George affectionately nuzzled his pocket for the carrot he knew was in there. The future terrified him—getting up each day to work at that mine, especially after the mine explosion. Playing baseball was all he ever wanted to do.

Chapter Four

1912

Joe spent any time away from the mine perfecting his baseball skills. When he couldn't find any of his friends or brothers to play with, he threw the ball against a wall at the mine to work on his arm and to practice catching ground balls at the same time. He practiced keeping his head and glove down. He threw strong and always gripped the ball on the seams. The best practices were when he could get someone to pitch to him so he could hit.

Joe's older brother, David, had been practicing his pitching skills and would pitch to Joe. David played on Meyersdale's town team on Sundays when he was not working at the mine. He brought Joe along with him whenever he could. Traveling to Meyersdale seventy miles away took several hours, so they set off early in the morning. They rode their bikes to the train station in Irwin. They took the interurban tram of the West Penn Railways over the mountains to Somerset, and then walked to Slicer Park in Meyersdale. Meyersdale's town team played against Connellsville and Uniontown, other small towns in southwestern Pennsylvania that also involved similar amounts of travel time on the tram.

Because they traveled on Sundays, Joe and David mixed with couples on dates, farmers and their wives taking an excursion to town, and commuters going to the baseball games. In between towns, the tram cars picked up speed and went 50 to 60 miles per hour. They went a little slower when they were climbing the steep grades of the mountains.

As they approached the tram with the other travelers, Joe loved the looks of the streamlined tram. It was painted glossy red with rows of windows at seat level. Its huge single headlight looked like a cyclops' eye.

"They are sleek. I like that there's no dust and smoke like the steam engines. We get enough foul air in the mines," David said.

"And I like that they move faster than my ol' cart with George," Joe said.

They paid their $1.25 round trip fare. When they got on the car, they moved through the wood-paneled cabin to one of the wicker seats and sat down. Joe immediately put his window down so he could feel the breeze on his face as they traveled.

On one of the Sundays, David and Joe met up with the other Meyersdale players, who called themselves the Bullies, to play against the Connellsville team. Joe watched from the stands as the game remained scoreless until the last inning due to David's pitching.

"Way to hold them, Pops," Joe yelled. David was in his late thirties and the rest of the town team players called him "Pops."

In the ninth inning, Meyersdale brought one man over home plate. Then they had the bases loaded when the Connellsville boys made a skillful double play and started to walk off the field. The player on third made it into home and the score was 2 to 0. The Connellsville team thought they had put three men out and wanted to repeat the play. The umpire declared the game over, and Meyersdale defeated the Connellsville team.

In the stands, where Joe was, the fans were not so graceful in defeat. Joe watched one of the fans punch an officer. Joe ducked his head and slipped past the fight unnoticed. He ran from the melee down to the field to congratulate his brother and head for home.

Joe considered himself lucky to have so many brothers who all liked baseball. His oldest brothers, Enoch and Jack, worked so hard at the mine and didn't really have time for leisure activities. Next oldest, Alexander, had married and moved out on his own to a small farm. But the four youngest brothers, David, William, James, and Thomas, delighted in playing. Joe took advantage of that, and they practiced together as much as they could. After being in the dark, damp mine most days, they derived great pleasure from being outside in the sunshine on grassy fields.

Thomas was finally old enough to take over for Joe with the donkey. Joe moved up to work the seams with his brothers. Joe became a breaster with William. Breasters worked in pairs on the horizontal veins of coal with pickaxes and hammers to leave behind open rooms. They left pillars of coal and rock to support the roof, and the area where they worked was like streets of a town. They walked for a mile underground to get to the seam where they were working. Water would gather in the lowest places, and the air was damp.

Although Joe missed his donkey, a canary replaced George. Joe and William took the canary with them every day. Joe named his bright yellow canary Sunny and whistled to his canary as he worked. And Sunny whistled back. If the canary fell off his perch or went to the bottom of his cage, Joe and William had time to put their respirators on and escape the shaft.

One bright spring day as Joe was riding his bike home from the town field where he and his brothers practiced, he saw a poster tacked to a faded brown fence post.

BASEBALL TRYOUT CAMP
ST. LOUIS BROWNS
POP KELCHNER
ONE DAY ONLY

Joe could hardly believe his eyes. This was another chance for him! He pedaled his bike as quickly as he could down the pot-holed road to tell his brothers.

"William? James?" he yelled. He jumped the six steps to the front porch and the wooden screen door slammed as he entered the house.

"What? Where's the fire?" Annie asked him. She pushed a few loose gray hairs back up into her bun as she swept the kitchen floor with a broom.

"Where are William and James?" Joe asked. His brothers appeared from the dining room into the kitchen when they heard Joe stomping and pacing.

"They're having a tryout camp!" Joe exclaimed, out of breath from biking down the street. He shifted his weight back and forth from one foot to the other. "We can all try out for this team."

"What team is it?" William asked.

"The St. Louis Browns," Joe replied.

"Just you should try out. You've been practicing so much," William said. "The rest of us aren't as good of players as you are, but David and I will go with you."

"No, William, we should all try out. Maybe we'll all get lucky," Joe said.

Joe could hardly stand to wait till the day of the camp. At meals with his family, Joe's foot tapped repeatedly on the floor under the table. If someone just looked his way, he would jump like a grasshopper. He oiled his glove and then would put his face right into the crease of it to smell the leather. His brother David caught him doing that one evening.

"That's not going to make you a better player, Joe," David joked.

"Don't make light of me," Joe said. Joe always thought of David as his smartest brother. David, eight years older than Joe, was the one who could do any math problem. When something broke in the house, David would take it apart and put it back together to fix it. He didn't need to become a baseball player like Joe did. He would always have his brains to fall back on. David worked in the mining office after he had designed and patented a new head lamp for the miners. Hopefully, the new headlamp would help stop the explosions that had killed so many miners in the last few years. Joe had even asked David to design a birdcage for Sunny with ventilation holes. If Sunny fell off his perch, Joe could close an airtight door over the ventilation holes and then he could revive him with oxygen from a small tank on the top of the cage.

The day finally arrived for the tryout. Joe and his two brothers showed up at the field.

Joe saw a tall man with a long, thin face handing out some uniforms and organizing the players into teams. He had a receding hairline, inky hair, and deep-set blue eyes. The man spoke to each prospective player with a Pennsylvania Dutch accent. Joe had heard some miners talking in the same manner, but the miners didn't speak in such an educated fashion as this man.

Joe was so excited, he ran up and introduced himself, "Good morning, sir. My name is Joe Harris. And these are my brothers, David and William."

"Charles Kelchner, but everyone callz me Pop," the man said.

"That's funny, Pop. They call my brother David here Pops when he plays," Joe said. David smiled as he watched Joe crack his knuckles, one by one, nervously.

"De shtudents at my university shtarted calling me Pop because zay say I am like a fazzer to zem. And de name shtuck. Pleazed to make your acquaintance, Pops, Villiam, und Joe. I haf heard of de Harris brozzers from Coulters," Pop said. "You are all coal minerz, correct?"

"We all work at the mine for now. David works in the office. William and I work the seams. But what we'd really like to do is play baseball," Joe answered.

'Vat position do you play?" Pop asked Joe.

"First base," Joe said. "David, here is a pitcher. He pitches for the Meyersdale town team called the Bullies. And William plays left field."

Kelchner unexpectedly threw his pencil at Joe's face. Joe's hand went up, and he snatched the pencil from the air before it could hit him.

"Gut reflexes. How old are you?" Pop asked.

"I'll be 21 next month, Pop," Joe replied. "David is 39 and William is 33."

"You are somewhat old for just shtarting out. But zose reflexes vill suit you vell on first base. Suit up and take your base," Pop said. "Bad news for you, David und Villiam, I can unnerstand how much you like baseball. Ve all do. Und I vould like to gif eferyone an audition. But you are much too old for our team und zere are so only many hours in ze day to look at the playerz who are eligible. Zank you for coming out."

Both David and William shook Pop Kelchner's hand. They would cheer for their brother.

Joe came out of the washroom behind the dugout wearing the wool baseball uniform and ran to first base. David and William watched from the third base line.

Kelchner eyed Joe from the dugout as the game started. Joe communicated with the other players and caught every ball that came to him. He tried not to repeat the mistakes he had made when he played the one game for the Tubers. When he got up to bat, he hit one triple and two doubles.

"Way to go, Joe," David yelled as he and William applauded each hit. Whenever Joe made contact with the ball, in his mind he was thanking his brother David for pitching to him so much.

Now that Joe had worked in the mine for years, he had filled out. He was 5 foot 10 inches tall and weighed 175 lbs. Each time he stepped up to bat, he pulled back his broad shoulders made tight and rigid from loading coal into buckets. He shouldered the bat with heavily muscled arms and gripped the bat with calloused hands used to swinging a pick. His legs were like tree trunks from years of walking George back and forth.

After the game, Kelchner talked to each player in the field office. Joe bit his lip as he waited for his turn. He drummed his fingers against his thigh.

"Harris, I like vat I zee in you. You haf a gift. You haf good flexibility. You are great on de short hop. You must haf really been practicing zat. Und you are a power hitter. But I already haf a great firsht baseman for the Browns. So, here is vat I'm going to do. I'm going to recommend you for anozzer team I scout for in Bay City, Michigan. Ve vill be in touch."

Chapter Five

1913

The letter arrived for Joe from Bay City in early February. Joe read it aloud to his family as they sat around the dinner table. Joe's sisters, who were married now and no longer lived at home, came over to hear the news.

"We enclose herewith a contract for the 1913 season with the Bay City Beavers for a salary of $750.00 to play first base and outfield. For your information, the pitchers and catchers will report to Bay City on Sunday, March 22, with the infielders and outfielders starting work on Friday, March 28. Upon receipt of your signed contract, I will send you transportation and detailed reporting instructions. With best wishes, I am, sincerely yours, Danny Jenkins, Manager, Bay City." Joe read.

Everyone at the table was quiet for a while. Then Enoch banged his open hand on the gingham tablecloth and started whooping and hollering. And the rest of the family joined in with laughter and congratulations. Joe's sisters, Mary and Margaret, hugged him.

"I'm proud of you, son," Joseph Sr. said. Joe had become the image of his father even down to the slight dimple in the middle of his chin. "You worked hard, and you never gave up."

"Thank you, Pop," Joe said, as his father took his turn to hug him and slap him on the back. "But I couldn't have done it without my brothers."

The third week of March seemed to arrive quickly. Joe was wearing his best suit on the train platform. "All aboard!" the conductor shouted. The huge locomotive swooshed into the busy station. The Pennsylvania Special was pulling four cars behind it. The train cars were painted forest green with beige frames around the windows. Joe could picture the train cars running through the blue mountains on the trip from Pennsylvania to Michigan.

"Well, this is it," Joe said to his mom and dad. Enoch, William, and Alex had come to see him off. Joe was wearing his straw hat to make himself seem a little taller. When Joe stood next to his over six-foot-tall brothers, he always felt so short. He hugged each brother on the track platform.

"We're gonna' miss you, boy," his father said as he shook his hand.

"I'm gonna' miss all of you, too, Pop. The Harris family has always been together. But this is a great chance for me," Joe said as he choked back his tears.

Joe turned to his mother and inhaled the smell of her floral perfume that she only wore for special occasions.

His mother was crying silently and embraced him so tightly he could barely breathe. None of her other children had ever wanted to venture so far from home. She knew Joe was her child with wanderlust. Neither one of them spoke.

Once aboard the train, he found a seat in his section. The seats were plush brown leather banquettes for two. He was sitting by himself, though, so he took a window seat. There was a shelf above his seat to store his bag. And above that there was another row of smaller windows that let in more light. A young family sat behind him, talking quietly.

He watched outside amazed as the telegraph poles rushed past. He had never been on a train like this one before and couldn't believe how fast it was going. Joe didn't even want to read the book he brought along—he was content to watch the countryside outside the window. ·

After a few hours, Joe headed through the jostling back door of his car to find the dining car. There were at least eight tables, each set for four people with crisp, white tablecloths. Each table had a colorful leaded glass table lamp on it. His mother would have loved the small leaded crystal salt and pepper shakers and the small leaded crystal cup of sugar cubes. A black waiter wearing an immaculate white shirt and tie with a floor length black apron handed Joe a menu. Puree of Tomatoes with Rice. Cold Consomme. Lake Trout aux Fine Herbs. Lobster a la Newburg. Larded Tenderloin of Beef Bordelaise. Roast Young Chicken Farsi. Chocolate Ice Cream or Roquefort for dessert. He felt like the coffee was the only thing on the menu he had tried before. He decided to have the chicken, chocolate ice cream, and a cup of coffee as they were the closest to what he was used to eating. He barely felt the train going around the curves in the track as he ate his dinner.

"That was certainly delicious chicken," Joe said to the waiter as he wiped his lips with his napkin. He felt like he should say something to the waiter because he was dining all alone. "Different from any chicken I've ever tasted."

"Yes, sir," the waiter replied automatically. "From what I understand, the chicken is marinated in lemon and yogurt over-night. Then that's wiped off and it's cooked on a grill."

"I don't believe I've ever had yogurt before," Joe said. "That must have been what made it taste so different."

"I can ask the chef to come out and talk to you about it, if you'd like," the waiter said, looking down at his towel folded over his arm and making no eye contact.

"Oh, that won't be necessary," Joe said. He was just trying to make some conversation but realized he was making the waiter uncomfortable. "Just tell him I thought it was great."

After dinner, Joe sought his berth in the sleeping car. A black porter in a pristine white jacket was making up the beds. There was a top and bottom bunk in each berth. A heavy, dark curtain separated each berth. Joe took the bottom bunk and went to sleep. If others were snoring around him, he didn't hear it. He was used to sleeping with others close by. He would arrive in Chicago in the morning.

In the morning after breakfast, Joe made his way to the last train car and stood on the platform. He looked at the shiny, straight rails behind him going off into the distance. Twenty-two years old and his life was changing.

After changing trains in Chicago, Joe finally arrived at the Pere Marquette depot in Bay City. It was a town very similar to Coulters where he grew up, but, instead of mining, this was a lumber town. Bay City was on the east side of the Saginaw River where it flowed into Lake Huron.

Joe walked a few blocks to the Saginaw River just to stretch his legs. His nose filled with the familiar smell of pulling a catfish up onto the bank amid rotting leaves. This river smelled so similar to the Youghiogheny River in Coulters. There was still snow on the ground even though it was March. Snow seemed to be welcome because the loggers with horse teams were skidding the logs on the snow and piling them next to the railroad tracks. Joe saw two young boys along the river putting ice down each other's backs. Then he walked back along Center Avenue until he found a small tourist hotel to spend the night. In the morning, he would look for a boarding house.

The next day, Joe found a huge house with white siding and green shutters. It had a small shingle in the fence with cursive writing: *Rooms for Rent.* He walked up to the door and knocked. "May I help you?" a small woman opened the door and asked.

"Ma'am, I'd like to rent one of your rooms." Joe said.

The woman let him into the foyer. The house was very similar to his two-story house in Coulters but without all the coal dust.

"I'll be playing baseball with the Bay City Beavers this season." Joe offered.

"It's $1.35 a night, and you pay a week at a time. You get a room with a bed and share a bathroom. The kitchen is for everyone. Dinner is at 6 o'clock." The woman said indifferently. She didn't seem to care that Joe was going to be a baseball player.

"I'll take it," Joe said.

As spring turned to summer, every day Joe headed to the baseball park to play first base. The park was only a few blocks from the boarding house, and Joe enjoyed the walk. What a difference he felt, walking to the ballpark rather than walking to the mine. He almost skipped to Clarkson Park. The fresh-cut grass and clay baselines with white chalked lines in front of the horseshoe shaped grandstand were home for him. Joe loved the feel of it when he dug his cleats into the dirt near the base.

Joe took first base and was ready to play for his new team. In his first game, the opposing team couldn't get a hit into the outfield, so Joe was busy defending his base. He caught ball after ball. He wished his brothers could see him, scanning the field like an eagle over a river, watching the pitcher.

Some teenage girls were standing along the fence by the free bleachers watching the game. "Isn't he just dippy?" he heard them giggle and say. Joe smiled to himself and blushed. Joe never had a girlfriend. He always concentrated on baseball.

When he got back to the boarding house, all the renters were sitting on the porch eating fresh peaches and ice cream. Somewhere down the street he could hear music playing. A man with a baritone voice was playing an accordion and singing. Joe started whistling along.

I've got an old mule, and her name is Sal.
Fifteen years on the Erie Canal.
She's a good old worker and a good old pal.
Fifteen years on the Erie Canal.
We've hauled some barges in our day.
Filled with lumber, coal, and hay.
And every inch of the way I know.
From Albany, to Buffalo.

Low bridge, everybody down.
Low bridge cause we're coming to a town.
And you'll always know your neighbor.
And you'll always know your pal.
If you've ever navigated on the Erie Canal.

Sitting on the porch with the other boarders reminded him of home, sitting around the kitchen table with his brothers and sisters. The song made him think of old George. Although it made him a little homesick, Joe thought he would like Bay City.

"You know what happened at the ballpark today?" Joe said to the other boarders to break the ice and start some banter.

One of the men boarders looked up from his ice cream to ask, "What happened?"

"The President of the South Michigan League called the police and had a couple of boys arrested. These young men steal balls that are knocked over the fences and then they sell them. I've knocked a few over the fences and seen them. They've stolen at least five balls every game. It's getting to be too expensive for the league to just let it go on like that," Joe said.

"Mmm, mmm, mmm," the boarder said as he shook his head and went back to eating his dessert. The man's response made him yearn for home even more. Joe's family at home would have been interested in listening to his baseball escapades.

Joe played all spring and into the summer. On July 3rd, the Bay City Beavers were set to play the Lansing Senators, a state rival. The day started like a typical workday for Joe, except this was a more festive occasion for Independence Day. Clarkson Park was decorated with red, white, and blue bunting. The Beavers were playing a doubleheader. Joe heard the mellow sounds of the brass band playing to entertain the crowd while he was in the locker room getting dressed. He smelled watermelon and popcorn. Joe was surprised when he entered the field, looked into the stands and saw that a couple of the boarders from his house came to the game to watch. In the first game, Joe drew a base on balls in the fourth inning. By that time, the Beavers were ahead 4 to 0. In the sixth inning, Joe sacrificed the third baseman to second base. He then scored on the center fielder's double. Joe looked up at the cheering fans as he crossed home plate. The Beavers won the game 7 to 0 when the left fielder hit a home run in the ninth. The Senators couldn't get a hit.

Joe was excited about playing the second game, but clouds swept in over the field and they dumped tons of water. The officials called the second game off in the first inning, but not before the rain drenched Joe. Water dripped off his cap down his neck. His wet uniform stuck to him. Joe saw the grandstand clearing out as the rain-soaked fans left the field. So much for an Independence Day celebration.

Chapter Six

1914

Joe wasn't in Bay City for long before he heard from the scout, Pop Kelchner, again on a bright, sunny day in May. Kelchner walked into the clubhouse at Clarkson Park and shook hands with a few of the other players. When he headed directly in Joe's direction, Joe thought to himself that something new was coming his way. In his heart, he knew he shouldn't get attached to one place as much as he enjoyed living in Bay City. If he became a baseball player—he would move around from city to city.

"Harris!" Pop exclaimed as if he was seeing an old friend again. Pop, wearing a suit and tie, had his dark hair parted down the middle and pomaded tight to his head. He seemed ready for business.

"Good to see you again, Pop," Joe said as they shook hands. "What brings you to Bay City?"

"I haf some gut newz for you. I can get you a tryout viz de New York Yankeez. But you must be at de Polo Grounds in New York in two veeks." Pop Kelchner told him seriously. "I haf already discuzzed zis with Mr. Jenkins. He is villing to gif

you a few veeks off. Und de Yankeez vill pay for your transportation."

Joe could hardly believe what he was hearing. He had a
chance to play for the major league.

The next day Joe walked back to the Pere Marquette train
station. He picked out the building from blocks away because
he remembered the pyramid-shaped tower on the roof. He
heard the steam engines chugging into the station. He dropped
his suitcase beside him and leaned against a wooden post of the
track platform as he waited. He saw some porters loading huge
bags of salt into the back of the train. On the departure board
overhead, he saw the white letters flap rapidly to show that his
train had arrived, and he boarded. A year ago, he had never
been out of Pennsylvania, and now he was riding trains all over
the country.

As the train approached New York City, Joe noticed more
and more tall buildings out the windows of the train. He saw a
woman hanging out colorful laundry on a line between two
buildings. When the train went over a low bridge, he saw a few
men playing cards on the street below. He saw children playing
in some water on the street. Little shops selling newspapers,
fruits and vegetables, and bread popped up in every block he
passed like jewels in a glass case. He watched a woman in a
blue dress walking a small poodle on a leash.

Joe took advantage of the first weekend to take a train into
Manhattan and walk around. He could hardly believe that this
boy from a small mining town was walking around a city full
of skyscrapers. He had to keep his eye on the cobblestones as
he walked so he wouldn't trip—but he kept looking up at all
the tall buildings. He excused himself every time he bumped
into someone on the sidewalk. Horses and buggies were clip-

clopping past him, and every once in a while, a motor car sputtered by. The cars honked when the horses got too close. Trolley cars clanged by. People spoke different languages and dressed in all different styles. He smelled chicken being fried mixed with the sewer and manure in the gutters. The smell of bread and coffee mingled with exhaust from the motor cars. The sparks from the trolley cars gave off a sulfur smell. Bright lights were all around.

Joe saw a painted sign for H & G Cohen in the Lower East Side of the city on Grand Street. He stepped down a few stairs into the small, basement linen shop and took a break from the cacophony of the city. He found a pair of beautifully embroidered pillowcases with open crochet lace work that he thought his mother would love. Annie would never spend the $2.50 on them for herself. Joe was making his own money now, so he had them shipped to Annie in Pennsylvania.

Joe was so preoccupied with sightseeing he didn't realize the sun was setting. He passed a restaurant that said it was open all night. Joe found it hard to believe that someone would need to eat in the middle of the night. But he had to get back to his hotel. They expected him at the ballpark in the morning.

The Polo Grounds was an amazing field, much larger than Clarkson Park in Bay City. The old wooden stadium had been destroyed by a fire a few years before—but now had been rebuilt and held over 30,000 fans for games. When Joe came off the elevated train platform at Eighth Avenue, he gazed at the new horseshoe-shaped grandstand tiers of concrete and steel. The roof was decorated with the coats of arms of all the National League teams. The aisle seats had iron scrollwork with a 'NY' emblem on them.

When Joe entered the clubhouse near the center field bleachers, he ran into a guy built just like him next to the deep wooden cubbies in the locker room. "Welcome." The guy stuck out his hand for a handshake. The stare Charlie gave Joe with his dark brown eyes unnerved him a little. It didn't match his warm demeanor. He was about the same height as Joe but a little thinner. "My name's Charlie Mullen. I just came from playing with the White Sox in Chicago."

"Joe Harris." Joe said as he shook his hand.

"I think we're trying out for the same spot on the team. First base. Where are you from?" Charlie asked as he knelt down to tie his shoes.

"I'm originally from the Pittsburgh area. But for the last year I've been playing in Bay City, Michigan," Joe said. Joe realized that this guy was already playing in the major leagues.

"That's close to Chicago!" Charlie exclaimed. "I'm originally from Seattle, Washington. I like Chicago, but not the cold winters. Seattle has rain, but not the cold. But I guess we go where we're paid to play."

"We've both traveled a far way to play this game." Joe said.

"At least it's not cold now, eh?" Charlie said. "We're lucky we got to be in New York in the sunshine."

It was a brilliant, clear day at the end of June when Joe got his chance at first base. The Yankees manager, Frank Chance, with one hand perched on the dugout railing, was watching. Joe picked from the row of wooden bats lying in front of the dugout for his only time at bat, and he struck out. Frank took Joe out and put Charlie into the game. The Yankees tied the Cleveland Indians 3 to 3. It was not a good game for Joe.

Frank and Joe talked in the dugout after the game. Joe couldn't help but stare at the interlocked NY on Chance's cap

and left sleeve. "Harris, I'll give you one more chance tomorrow," Chance said. "Kelchner says you're a power hitter and
heck of a first baseman. We're in the cellar of the American
League, and we need every player to pull his weight. The only
team that's worse than us right now is Cleveland, and we just
tied with them."

"I understand, Mr. Chance," Joe said. "I'm going to give it
my all."

Joe was staying at a hotel in the Bronx and had a hard time
falling asleep that night. Not only was he hearing sirens and
people talking outside his hotel room, which he rarely heard in
Bay City, but also he kept replaying the game in his head. He
had to do well in the next game or the job would go to Charlie. Joe tried to close his eyes and picture himself making
plays. He had to dig deep for this.

At the next game Joe tried to do everything right, but his
nerves seemed to get in his way. He was running the bases
when he got a hit. A pop-up fly ball came right to him, but he
didn't catch it. It plopped into the clay right beside the first base
bag.

"Aaah!" Joe huffed in frustration as he picked up the ball
and threw it back to the pitcher. At that moment, Joe knew in
his heart they were sending him back to Bay City.

"Harris, I'll see you in my office," Frank Chance said to him
as the players were leaving the field.

When Joe got to his office, Chance said, "I'm going to have
to give the first base slot to Mullens. That boy is game to the
core. I'm rather glad that he had to face the fire with you. It
showed me what was really in him."

"I appreciate you giving me an opportunity," Joe said. "No
excuses, but I really feel like my nerves got the best of me."

Joe went directly to the locker room after his meeting with the manager. "Well, I think we know who is getting the first base position," Joe said to Charlie as he shook his hand. "Congratulations. It's well deserved."

"Thank you, Joe," Charlie said. "What are you going to do now?"

"Head back to Michigan. But I'm going to spend a week or two in the big city first. I've never been anywhere like this," Joe said.

Why had he been so nervous? Was the big city throwing off his game? He stayed in New York for another week to see what their Independence Day celebration was like. He had never been in such a place for Independence Day and needed something to buoy his spirits. It had to be better than getting drenched in a rainstorm like he did last year in Bay City.

On the morning of July 4th, the first thing Joe wanted to do was head to the carousel in Central Park. He heard that the carousel was a new steam-powered one. An earlier one had been powered by a blind mule walking in an underground pit, which sadly reminded him of old George. Joe was delighted to see so many brightly painted animals and two chariots and the gleaming paint not dulled by coal dust. Although he was no longer a child, but because he hadn't had much of a childhood, Joe was dead set on riding. He had to choose what animal he wanted to ride. The lion, the boar, or one of the magnificent horses? Joe couldn't help but smile feeling the slight breeze when his black steed, adorned in red and gold saddle and bridle, rose and fell as it went around and around.

A young girl was riding the white horse directly in front of Joe. A woman only a few years older than Joe, probably her mother, was standing beside her. She kept glancing back at Joe. He felt like he had to say something.

"I never got to do this before," Joe yelled to be heard over the calliope music.

"Tsk, tsk. You're being a bit of a simp, but if you don't bother us, we won't bother you," the woman replied, and she turned back to her little girl and put her arm around her protectively.

Joe thought to himself, That's a real New Yorker.

Joe left the park and squeezed into the crowd along Fifth Avenue to see the parade with dozens of colorful floats, decorated with red, white, and blue streamers. One float carried two women. One stood completely still as the teal green Statue of Liberty. The other was dressed as Lady Columbia, the personification of the United States, wearing a red and white striped dress with a blue shawl and enthusiastically waving an American flag. When a marching band came down the street, he loved that thudding feeling in his chest when the bass drum sounded, and then the snare drums passed slowly. He could smell meat barbecuing. Joe was sweating through his shirt as he walked farther down the street where an ice man had set up a huge block of ice. Shirtless kids were laughing and crowding in close to lick the big block. Joe bought himself an ice cream cone from a street vendor, although he wanted to crowd next to the ice block along with the kids.

That evening Joe watched the fireworks on the Williamsburg Bridge. The fireworks illuminated the bridge in a waterfall of red, orange, blue, and green with the city skyline behind it. The 40-story Municipal Building with its grand cupola in black relief towered over all the other buildings. Joe oohed and ahhed along with the rest of the crowd at each burst and crackle of color in the black sky. Joe was happy he stayed in the city and was certain he would have seen nothing like this in Coulters or even in Pittsburgh.

Chapter Seven

1915

Rumors from the front office that he would be traded again circulated around the clubhouse when Joe returned to Bay City. He had to get used to this life of constant changes because that was what playing professional baseball was like. He was a rolling stone and had to go where the game said he must go.

Bay City traded him to the Chattanooga Lookouts and Chattanooga, Tennessee, would be his new home. The Lookouts had a fan contest to select their name, and the winning fan thought the team should be named after Lookout Mountain. Joe got a book from the library to research his new city. He read that the name for Chattanooga came from the Cherokee and meant "two mountains looking at each other."

Joe walked past Andrews Field on East Third Street. He had to find a new place to live and wanted to be close to the ballpark, but he also realized the ballpark was next to the busy rail yard and he didn't want to hear trains all night long. Joe came across a boarding house several blocks away at 332 East Third Street. His boarding house in Bay City had been at 332 as well. This coincidence meant this must be the house for him.

Joe went up to the door and knocked. An elderly woman who reminded him of his grandmother answered the door. She was much shorter than him, had curly blue-grey hair, and was wearing a patched apron smock over her plain cotton dress. "I'm looking to rent a room here. Do you have any rooms available?" Joe asked.

The woman smiled and invited him into the parlor. "Please take a seat. I have one room with a small twin bed. And it comes with dinner every evening."

"I'll take it," Joe said without even looking at the room. This place just felt right to him.

"Maybe we should introduce ourselves first. My name is Emily Harding." The older lady sat in a worn velvet armchair and motioned for Joe to sit across from her.

"I'm Joe Harris. You remind me of the pictures I've seen of my grandma in Scotland, Mrs. Harding. My mum told me she was always afraid of my grandma, but you don't seem scary to me. You also remind me of the lady who ran the boarding house in Bay City, but much nicer. I'm gonna be playing baseball for the Lookouts this season." Joe said. It seemed like he had just said a similar thing to the boarding house owner in Bay City.

"Oh, my! How exciting to have a ball player staying here. I didn't know what kind of work you did, but you stand up so straight and tall. I don't think you have any reason to fear me, dear!" Mrs. Harding exclaimed as she clapped her hands together.

Joe smiled. He was looking forward to staying here.

The next day Mrs. Harding showed an article in the newspaper to Joe when he got home. It said that Joe Harris was a "phenom." And that he would be a great first sacker for the Lookouts.

"Look at this, Mr. Harris," Mrs. Harding said. "You're in the paper!"

Joe blushed and said, "Mrs. Harding, those are awful nice things for the reporters to say. But I really need the experience of a minor league team for a year or so. Then I want to get up to play in the majors. And you can call me, Joe."

Joe had been eking out a living with the Class B Lookouts for several weeks. They rode from city to city on the train. The team usually played cards on the train and at the platform to pass the time. They asked Joe to join them.

Jimmy Johnston, the left fielder, was the first to ask him. "Joe, do you want to come and join us in a game of rummy?"

"Thanks for the invite," Joe said. "You know, Jimmy, I like watching you steal bases when we play."

"I try to steal to give us an edge, Joe," Jimmy said as he dealt out the cards. "I learned from my brother, Doc. He plays baseball, too."

"Any pointers you can give me I would be happy to take," Joe said. "I know you stole over a hundred bases. And a couple of my brothers play ball, too. But not professionally."

Jimmy grinned as he plopped the cards down in front of each player.

"Jimmy's the hometown hero, too," Kid Elberfeld said. Kid was the Lookout's short stop. "From Cleveland, Tennessee. Just down the road."

Kid Elberfeld was one of the smallest players on the team at only 5' 7", but his temper made up for his size. Because Joe played first base, he had been on the receiving end of his explosive arm. Kid was fearless in turning double plays and was often spiked.

"Why do they call you, Kid? I mean, you're 40 years old," Joe asked, tempting Kid's bad temper.

Kid seemed to be in a good mood with the card game. "They started calling me, Kid, when I left school early."

"Who hasn't left school early?" Joe asked. "I had to leave in the 8th grade and go work in the mines."

"There were 11 kids in our family in Ohio," Blonde haired, blue eyed Kid said. "We couldn't afford for us to all go to school. Some of us had to work."

"Me, too!" Joe's mouth fell open in surprise. "I have seven brothers and two sisters."

Fred Graff had joined the team two years earlier and played third base. His teammates all sighed and rolled their eyes when he said, "Joe, let me tell you a story about the time I made the winning run against Birmingham."

"Okay, Fred," Joe said.

"Burleigh Grimes was pitching. He used to be on the Lookouts with us. He saw me come up to bat, and he tried to intentionally walk me. I could see it in his eyes. I just waited for him to throw me one a little on the inside, and I drove in the winning run!" Fred said.

"That's something, Fred," Joe said as he put his dealt cards in numerical order in his hand.

"He was so mad! At the end of the game, he grabbed that baseball and threw it right over the grandstand!" Fred laughed. Jake Pitler, the second baseman, and Jud Daley, the center fielder, laughed along with him.

"This is only the hundredth time we heard this story," Jake whispered to Joe.

At that moment, Jake wolf whistled. Two of the other players were walking along the train platform to join the card game.

The taller of the two men was dressed in a dark pinstriped suit with a stylish bowler hat on his head. His oxford shoes glistened with polish. Joe could see a glimmer of a gold watch chain dangling from his pocket.

"Hey, Rube," Jake said. "You don't have to show us all up by dressing like that. We're just heading out to play a ball game." Rube Marshall was the team's pitcher. Not only did he dress better than any of the other players, he also had the best work ethic. Joe heard at one time he had pitched 23 innings in one game.

The other man who arrived with Rube had a thick shock of dark hair and deep-set eyes. He was Pop Kitchens, the catcher.

"Let me tell you another little fun story from behind the plate," Pop said to Joe as he and Rube sat down at the card game. "Reddy Mack used to be our second baseman. He used to carry a boiler room whistle in his back pocket. He would blow that whistle at various times during the game, especially when an umpire made a rotten call. You know the ump stands right behind me, Silk O'Loughlan. He was furious. Had a temper just like Kid. He told him to put that whistle up. But Reddy says, 'There's no rule laid down telling me to cease and desist.' So, he kept blowin' that whistle whenever he wanted."

Joe laughed at all their stories. He enjoyed being part of this team.

It wasn't long before Joe found out for himself about Umpire O'Loughlan in a game against the Nashville Volunteers. Joe was playing third base and it was the ninth inning. The Volunteers' first baseman Dave Callahan led off by walking. He was sacrificed to second base by shortstop Dolly Clark and cleverly stole third base.

"Safe," Silk O'Loughlan said, crossing and extending his arms several times, when Callahan tagged the third base bag.

"Come on, Silk," Joe said. "I tagged him."

"I listen for the thud and the pop," Silk said. "He's safe."

Catcher Gabby Street grounded to Rube Marshall, and Callahan was caught off third base. He circulated back and forth quite freely for a while but was finally rolled in the dirt and touched out by Joe. Joe was miffed because Umpire O'Loughlan had erred grievously in calling Callahan safe at third base on that steal just before.

Now Joe had a story for the next card game. Despite this great team with their considerable expertise and appreciable comradery, the Lookouts played poorer than any other team in their league. Joe was their only consistent hitter.

He sent a postcard home to his family in Coulters. The front had a picture of the steep incline railway up Lookout Mountain in Chattanooga.

"Dear Mum and Pop, It's hard for me to believe that I've moved again. I'm living in Tennessee now. It reminds me a little bit of home with the mountains and the river. Doesn't the incline on this postcard look like the one in Pittsburgh? I miss all of you. Your son, Joe."

Joe liked to walk along the Tennessee River to the ballpark from home. It reminded him of the Youghiogheny River in Coulters, and the sound of the rushing water also helped him clear his head. Joe knew they had traded him to improve his stats. He felt like his swing was getting too big. He would try to relax his hands and see if that would make his swing better.

When Joe got home from practice on an early summer day in May, he joined the rest of the boarders in Mrs. Harding's dining room. They were listening to the radio before they had dinner. A German U-boat had sunk the passenger ship, Lusitania. American lives were lost but President Wilson wanted to keep the United States out of the war in Europe.

"All those poor people drowned," Mrs. Harding whispered through tears.

The radio announcer said that 128 of the passengers who died were Americans.

"This is just awful," one of the other boarders said. "There were women and children on that ship."

Joe bowed his head. "This is disgusting. A crime. We'll have to get into the war with those Jerrys.'"

The next day, when Joe went to the ballpark to practice, he looked up at the American flag and thought about the Lusitania again. He kept seeing the tears roll down his dear landlady's face. His mother was probably shedding tears in Pennsylvania, too. He had to put those images out of his head. He had to concentrate on improving all of his stats. He continued to improve on his hitting.

At a game one June afternoon, the announcer said, "Look at that Harris hit! He hits just like the cannon that shot the spaceship to the Moon in that old movie *A Trip to the Moon*!"

Joe smiled when he heard that because he could picture the image of that moon from the French movie. He had seen it years ago, but it was so interesting that everyone remembered it. The crusty moon in the film had a human face. Advertisers used the image for everything from selling soda pop to furniture.

The next time Joe came up to bat, the announcer said, "Here comes Joe Harris, the Moon, up to bat! Let's see if he hits one to the moon again today!"

As Joe headed home that day, he came upon Mr. Ciccolino, the old Italian man who sold ices outside of the ballpark. "I-

Cee, I-Cee," he would yell. He scooped the ice into a paper cone from his old wagon and flavored it with lemon syrup. Mr. Ciccolino smiled as he presented Joe with his ice and said, "Ciao, Joseph!" or should I say, "Ciao, Moon!" Joe laughed.

Soon Joe's hitting had improved so much that he was now consistently a .300 hitter—a magic number. He wrote home to his parents again to tell them he had even received a pay raise from the Lookouts and he would be able to send some money home to them. Joe had to focus on his hitting constantly to earn that new increased income. He had to stay mentally tough.

In a game with Memphis, the fans huzzahed Joe repeatedly. Joe got two slashing doubles and a triple. Soon the whole stadium was chanting, "Moon! Moon! Moon!" whenever he would get up to bat.

Despite Joe's success, the team continued to lose. In July, Moose McCormick, their manager, quit. Kid Elberfeld took his place.

McCormick spoke to the press. "Yes, I decided, the best thing I could do for the club was to step out. Goodness knows I have done my best. I have tried to pick my pitchers carefully. I have attempted every trick I know to break a batting slump. I have used all the baseball knowledge and personal appeals I could make to get some winning ball playing out of the club, but I have failed to produce."

McCormick continued. "Somebody had to bear the burden of the team's many defeats, and it was inevitable that it should be the manager. I have no criticism to make of the players. I would not accuse one of them of failing to stand by me. The fans have roasted me, I know. The fans want and love a winner, and I don't blame them."

From September 9th to the 14th, with Kid Elberfeld at the helm, the Lookouts compiled seven consecutive shutouts with pitchers George Cunningham, Mudball Clark, and Rube Marshall racking up 53 scoreless innings. But on September 15th, the Mobile Gulls' left fielder tripled to right with Rube's first pitch in the first game to end their streak. The Lookouts had early leads in both games of the doubleheader but could not hold on. Clark gave up the second game.

In the sixth inning of the second game, the bases were loaded. When the Gulls' catcher walked, it forced their centerfielder home. Kid Elberfeld flew to within inches of the umpire's face, leaning into him. "Come on, O'Toole," he yelled at the umpire, spit flying. "That was a perfect strike! And now you're going to let him walk?"

"You're out of here," O'Toole ejected the new manager from the field.

The Gull's pitcher singled to center for the final run that drove the nail into the coffin. The club from Mobile, Alabama, ended the Lookout's streak on the 15th, serving Chattanooga two consecutive losses in the doubleheader. Another story for the boys to talk about on their next train ride.

Chapter Eight

1917

Joe was now batting .305 after playing with the Lookouts for two years, and it looked like he would be moving yet again.

"Harris, I need to see you in my office," Kid Elberfeld said. Elberfeld intimidated Joe now that he was the manager of the team. He was known as the Old Tobasco Kid of the big leagues because he had such a bad temper. Joe wanted to show Kid the respect he deserved as a manager, but he couldn't help himself. He still called him Kid and not Mr. Elberfeld.

"Did you realize that you were wearing your pants inside out when you took the field yesterday?" Kid asked him.

Joe turned bright red in the face. He was so intent on improving his game that he hadn't noticed that at all. Sometimes he was absent-minded that way, though. Baseball was all that mattered to him. It surprised him that not one of the players had mentioned it to him, and they let him play the whole game that way.

"That's not why I called you in here," Kid laughed at Joe's red face. Sometimes Kid would joke around with Joe, just like

the beginning days when he was the shortstop and not the manager of the team. "You're moving up to the big leagues."

Joe could hardly contain his feelings. He puffed up his chest
as he went from feeling embarrassed to feeling proud.

"How do you feel about moving to Cleveland?" Kid asked.

"Cleveland isn't very far from Pittsburgh," Joe exclaimed.
"I'd love to be closer to my family. It's a great city. Although,
I've loved living in Chattanooga."

"That's what I thought you would say. The Indians like what
they see in you. Now that you're batting .305, they're willing
to take a chance on you. I told them you would be one of the
best first basemen in the league by the end of the season. I'll be
sorry to lose you."

"Funny story about the Indians that I just heard. You know,
Joe, they used to be called the Naps, after their star player, Na-
poleon Lajoie. But after so many years of poor pitching, I read
in the paper that they were called the Naps because they folded
so easily. Like a napkin. Isn't that priceless? But they're doing
much better now. Kind of middle of the league. They're getting
some good players, and that could change things for them in
the future. I count you as one of the good ones."

"Thank you, Kid. I'll try to do you proud. I've been hunting
practically all winter during the off season. I think I've done
enough to keep off the fat. I won't have a chance to say good-
bye to the guys. Would you tell them for me?" Joe said as he
walked out of the office. Joe turned his head around and winked
at Kid. "And they won't be folding so much with me on the
team."

Joe remembered his short tryout with the Yankees a few
years ago. He knew that this second chance with the Indians

was a big one, and he would try to do everything he could not to blow the opportunity.

The August sun was beating down on him when he stepped out of the Cleveland train station. Joe found a hotel to stay in for a few nights right on Euclid Avenue. He wanted to explore the city, but it was so hot outside. Joe thought he would step into a movie theatre to cool off. Joe bought himself a Coke at the snack bar, went into the dark theatre, and sank into the deep velvet seat.

Before the movie started playing, the song "Over There!" came through the speakers of the theatre. Then President Wilson came on the news service to talk about the war in Europe and the draft. President Wilson called it Selective Service. The President wanted all eligible American men to volunteer.

Joe thought about Mrs. Harding and the other boarders at the boarding house in Chattanooga and how upset they had been at the news of the Lusitania sinking. News reports said that German U-boats were patrolling along the eastern coast of the United States. Joe was torn. He wanted to play baseball and was finally getting his chance with a major league team, but he also wanted to serve his country.

The next day Joe ventured east from his hotel to the Hough neighborhood to find League Park. His clothes stuck to him in the humidity. He could smell the fisheries of Lake Erie and thought briefly about buying himself a swimming costume. Going into the lake for a swim might be another way to cool off in the August heat.

In the clubhouse at League Park, Joe ran into a man who looked more like a boxer than a baseball player. He was a stocky man with a flattened nose and square smile.

"Steve O'Neill, it is," the man introduced himself. "I'm the catcher."

"Joe Harris," Joe said as he shook the man's huge hand. "They traded me here. I'll be playing first base. I know who you are, Steve. You're in all the newspapers. You're one of the best catchers in the game."

"Ye are in the newspapers sure, too, Joe. What they don't say in the papers is that I grew up in a minin' town near Scranton. I used to get paid a few pennies a day to separate the slate from the coal. Baseball was a way out of that life for me, me lad," Steve said in his Irish accent.

"For me, too!" Joe exclaimed as he thought back to the conversation he had with Kid Elberfeld about their similar childhoods. "My brothers and I worked in the mines in Coulters, outside of Pittsburgh. At first, I tended the donkeys. Then I moved up to work the seams. I love animals and liked taking care of my little donkey, but baseball is my dream. My brothers still work there."

"How big is your family?" Steve asked.

"We had 10," Joe said. "Enoch, Jack, Alexander, David, William, James, and Thomas are my brothers. Thomas is my baby brother, but he, David, and William played some baseball with me. Mary and Margaret are my sisters. Alexander is the only one who doesn't work in the mines. He got married and bought a farm."

"Thirteen for myself, a baker's dozen," Steve said with a wink. "I won't name 'em all to yourself, now. Some of my brothers play ball, too. Jack, Mike, and Jim."

"I want to play baseball in the worst way. But I also think I need to help fight this war," Joe said.

"Ay. My family came from Ireland. They're closer to the fightin' than we are here. Sure and I think us baseball players could throw more gas bombs in an hour than those Jerrys could throw in a week. There we go now," Steve said. Joe and Steve headed out to the field for practice. Joe thought they were going to become fast friends.

Joe didn't have to wait long for his chance to serve. When he arrived at the clubhouse one day to start practice, some men from the Draft Board were already there. They were signing up all the players for Selective Service. They examined Joe along with the others.

The easiest requirement for Joe to pass was that he was over the 5' 6" minimum height requirement. Along with the medical and eye test, they also gave Joe a literacy test. It started out with easy yes or no questions:

Do dogs bark?

Is coal white?

Then it got a little more difficult:

Does water run uphill?

Are stamps used on letters?

Do 100 cents make a dollar?

Are attempted suicides always fatal?

And near the end of the test, there were some questions where Joe, who had only completed grammar school, had to guess at the answers:

Are exulted positions held by distinguished men?

Do thieves commit depredations?

Are intermittent sounds discontinuous?

Are pernicious pedestrians translucent?

A thin gentleman with the Draft Board stood up to talk to the players when their exams were finished. "We are recruiting you for the 320th Infantry of the 80th Division. You will see combat, but you will also play baseball to keep up morale for the troops. It's an important job to keep up the mens' spirits. You will play out the rest of this season with the Indians, but as soon as the season is over, you'll be reporting to Camp Lee in Virginia for basic training. You are being recruited to serve out the full length of the war."

When the Draft Board spokesman finished talking, Lee Fohl, the Indians' manager, stepped up to speak. A tall but stocky man, he had been a catcher before becoming the manager.

"All of you who have stepped up to serve will have a place on the team when you return," Fohl said in his quiet, calm manner. "We're proud of what you're doing. In the meantime, we will trim the team to 20 members until this war is over. And we'll be changing the schedule to reduce mileage as much as possible. Save gas for the troops."

Fohl stepped back, and his friend, Tris Speaker, addressed the team. Speaker had the sleeves rolled up on his shirt, and it was damp in spots from the heat. Speaker was one of the best center fielders in baseball. Although Fohl was the manager, he did nothing without Speaker by his side.

"Lee is right. We have to defend the world and who better to do it than the men of baseball," Speaker bellowed. "Let's whip the Kaiser! Uncle Sam needs us!" The men in the locker room all cheered.

The newspaper sports reporters were waiting for them when they finished the meeting. They wanted to report on which men were going over to fight the Germans. Out of all the players on the Cleveland club, six were eligible for the draft and were probably going to be called into service at the end of the season. Joe was one of the six.

In October, the Indians traveled to Chillicothe, Ohio to play an exhibition game against the Cincinnati Reds for the troops at Camp Sherman.

"Joe, would you be wantin' to go out and see what the night-life is like here before the big game tomorrow," Steve asked.

"I don't really drink," Joe answered.

"Well, we need to be changin' that," Steve said. "I'm very Irish, very Catholic and very patriotic but I can out-drink any man."

"Where will we find a saloon?"

"We're not going to a saloon. For sure, we're headin' to the Officers' Club on Paint Street. Ye just come along with me, lad," Steve said.

Joe and Steve walked down the street until they found the unmistakable Wissler Building, a red brick storefront with a large cross on the center window and two side windows that looked like lollipops. A doorman stopped them at the entrance. Enlisted men were not allowed to enter.

"We be Steve O'Neill and Moon Harris of the Cleveland Indians and we'd like to come in," Steve said.

"Yes, sir," the doorman said.

"Two beers, mate," Steve said to the bartender as they sidled up to the bar. Soon Joe and Steve were surrounded by a sea of brown service coats, breeches and boots. When the officers of Camp Sherman found out that Joe and Steve were famous base-ball players, the beer and whiskey flowed.

The next morning, Joe woke groggily in the barracks dor-mitory that the team was sharing. He didn't remember how they got back there.

"I'm thinkin' ye might have taken a drop too much," Steve said from across the room. "Get in the shower and sober up so we can head to the game."

Before the game started, Joe, Steve, Tris Speaker, and a few of the other Cleveland players threw a dozen balls into the masses of soldiers watching them from the hillside west of the field. The Cleveland club shouldered its bats and marched in military order before Major General Glenn. The Major General then shook each player's hand. While the clubs were taking batting practice, scores of officers and men shook hands with the various players. Just before the game opened, they presented a baseball bearing all the players' autographs to Major General Glenn who afterwards threw out the first pitch.

During the game, when a foul ball was hit into the crowd, a squad of troops fell on it. The men would even run out onto the field and block Tris from fielding balls and then scurry back to the sidelines.

It thrilled Joe to do his part to help win the game. In the second inning, he walked and then went around the bases on singles by two of the other Cleveland players. Then, in the fourth, he hit into the crowd for three bases and scored on a fly to center. "Moon, Moon, Moon!" the soldiers chanted. Cleveland won 3 to 1, and he had been responsible for two of the runs. Joe wanted to fight, but he would also be proud to play baseball for the soldiers if that was where he was needed.

Chapter Nine

Early 1918

In February, Joe headed to Camp Lee in Newport News, Virginia. When he got off the train, he couldn't believe how many bleached canvas tents he saw. There were rows and rows of them as far as he could see, like a yard full of fluffy dandelion tops waiting to be blown into the wind.

After Joe found his tent and his bunk, he headed over to the stable area. Camp Lee was the debarkation site for the cavalry, too. He heard the horses whinnying as he walked through the damp mud. Joe had kept an apple from his lunch in his pocket. He found a big bay gelding in the first stall. He shared his apple. The gelding was more handsome but still reminded him of his donkey, George, back at the mine when he was a kid. He had come a long way from that kid in Coulters. Now he was 27 years old and getting ready for war.

Each day started at 5:45 a.m. when the bugler blew reveille. After an hour of calisthenics, Joe spent mornings at the shooting range. There was a lot of kick from the rifle, and the noise was considerable. Joe's ears were ringing, and there were only four soldiers shooting at once. Joe tried to imagine what it would be like with hundreds shooting. Later in the day they would hike for several miles. Sixteen-hour days were common, and Joe felt stronger every day.

It was June before they scheduled Joe to ship out. He wiped the sweat from his brow with a handkerchief.

"This is some humidity," he mumbled under his breath to himself. He could hardly wait to get to Europe and fight.

He left Virginia on a troopship with 1400 other men. Joe noticed 10 other ships in his convoy. It was so miserably hot that he tried to sleep on the deck whenever he could. Joe missed having a daily newspaper to read to keep up on baseball back home. He tried to exercise on deck to keep in condition, but it was so crowded. Food was wholesome and plentiful, and Joe could keep it down after the first couple of days when his sea-sickness had subsided. But overall, it was a dismal voyage. Joe continually thought about the German U-boats beneath the waves, the same boats that sunk the Lusitania.

After five weeks at sea, Joe finally landed in Le Havre, France. Just like the seas of canvas tents in Camp Lee, this time there were seas of brown-capped doughboys on the docks. The drill sergeants marched the soldiers to their barracks.

When Joe got inside and found his cot, he found the guy who would share the top bunk. He was much taller than Joe, a little over six foot. He was also much thinner. He had dark, piercing eyes and wavy, dark hair.

The man stuck out his hand, "Johnny Miljus. I believe we'll be playing baseball together. I'm part of the 320th, too."

"Joe Harris," Joe replied. "I just came from the Cleveland Indians."

"Wow," Johnny said. "I play minor league ball in Toledo with the Mudhens. I heard of you, though. I read about you in the papers. Don't they call you 'the Moon'?"

Joe's cheeks burned because he was still a little embarrassed at all the fanfare over his recent fame with the Cleveland team.

"Yes, they call me that," Joe said.

"They call me the 'Big Serb,'" Johnny laughed. "I grew up in Pittsburgh, in Lawrenceville. I worked in steel mills in the summers when I was home from school."

"I grew up in Coulters," Joe said. "Close to Pittsburgh. I worked in the mines before I got into baseball. I don't want to go back there, ever. I want to play ball."

But there was no time for baseball now. They loaded Joe and Johnny into a boxcar and headed to the town of Verdun in France. There was standing room only on the boxcars, and Joe thought he would pass out from the smell of so many fearful and jittery men packed together. Joe was relieved when they arrived. At least in the barracks there was room to move about. He began trench training with the French forces the next day.

After only a week of training in improvised trenches, learning to put on the gas mask, to throw grenades and to thrust their bayonets, Joe and Johnny were ready to march to the Argonne Forest and to fight in the real trenches.

They had seen nothing like these dense woods back in Pittsburgh. The trees soared to the sky, but their trunks had all been burnt black by years of fighting. There were huge craters crisscrossed with barbed wire and entanglements in the sweeping fields.

The French trenches were filled with mud, rats, and lice. They were about eight feet deep and went in a zig zag pattern. Joe found that he had to bail out the water with a bucket every morning or the piles of sandbags that he slept on would be wet at night. There was no lighting a fire, not even a match, as that would draw German sniper fire. For the few hours that he slept, he went to bed wet and woke up wet. He put empty sandbags over his boots to try to keep them warm and dry, but it was futile. Most of the day Joe felt very bored as most of the fighting went on right at dusk. Joe carried a flask of whiskey with him and took a swig when no one was looking.

Sometimes when Joe would fall asleep, he would think he was back in the mine. The trenches and bunkers reminded him of the gaping dark mine entrance. Then he would jolt awake.

"Johnny?" he whispered. "You awake?"

"Yeah, Moon?" Johnny replied.

"I can't sleep," Joe said.

"Just look up at the stars and think about our friends back home looking up at those same stars," Johnny said. "Someday we'll be back home, sitting with them under the same stars at the same time."

"And don't forget about the moon," Joe said. "We'll sit under the moon."

Johnny chuckled quietly and adjusted himself on his sandbag to try to get an hour or two of sleep. The moon shone down on both of them.

Clouds of poisonous gas would often drift into the trenches without warning. Joe would see the blue fog coming and quickly put on his gas mask. All night long shells exploded, lighting up the sky and filling the air with dust and smoke. He could feel the earth rumble under him during the shelling.

They had only been in the trenches for a week when one evening they were ordered to take a German machine gun in a pillbox across the field from their position. Joe and the rest of the platoon scrambled up out of the trenches into the field in front of them. There was a barrage of artillery shelling, both from the Germans and from their own side. Joe hunkered down in a shell hole along the way. In a flash of shell fire, he saw the shadow of a German soldier as he bayoneted Johnny in the shoulder before Joe could get to him. Fueled by adrenaline, Joe's hands trembled as he shot the German soldier. Joe had hunted and shot deer before, but he had never seen a man die. He wanted to cover his eyes with his hands but there was no time for that. He crawled through the mud to get to his friend.

"Just leave me here," Johnny said through clenched teeth. "I'll make it back by myself."

"I'm not leaving you," Joe said, breathing heavily. Joe dragged Johnny over the body of the German soldier and back to the log-lined trench. The medics marked the wounded with tags. A red tag meant that you were to be sent home. A yellow tag meant you went back to the front. Johnny's tag was red.

Joe backed away from Johnny and the medics and readied himself to mount the wooden ladder out of the pit and return to the battle. He felt dirt spatter on his face when a sniper's bullets hit into the ground above him and he ducked for cover. The lieutenant next to him was not so lucky when he was cut down by the sniper and his body fell limp on top of Joe. Joe climbed out from under the lieutenant's body and pushed himself a few feet away. He leaned his face against the mud wall of the trench and sobbed. He tried to catch his breath. The lieutenant was someone's brother. Someone's son. Joe missed his mother and thought how crushed she would be if German soldiers killed him.

After those two weeks of combat, headquarters made Joe a sergeant.

Joe had a young man in his platoon who shook with every nerve in his body. He had probably lied on his enlistment papers because he looked to be only sixteen or seventeen years old. Joe called most of his men by their last names, but he called this boy by his first name, Jeff, because he was so young. His eyes bulged out of his head. He had dark, almost black, wiry hair. He continually took off his helmet and ran his fingers through it nervously. Joe could tell he was terrified. And yet, he volunteered for every mission.

"I know I'm not coming back, Sergeant Moon. I just feel it," he said. "So, send me and save these other guys." All the men in the platoon called Joe 'Sergeant Moon' instead of 'Sergeant Harris.'

"Jeff, I appreciate that you always volunteer. But let's just see what tomorrow brings." Joe told him. He tried to calm him down when Joe didn't feel calm himself. The German machine gunner and sniper kept them trapped in the trench for days.

It wasn't long before Joe got an answer to their captive situation. He couldn't tell what he was seeing exactly that evening. It was a black animal, but it looked like it had wings and a slender, sloped head with huge eyes. When it finally got close to him in the trench, he realized it was a dog, a black greyhound. The dog was wearing a gas mask and had a pack with baskets on each side. On his collar was his name Lucifer. Attached to his collar was a message asking Joe to have his men hold their position. In each basket was a pigeon. The French had put a message in a cylinder around the neck of each pigeon with the location of the German machine gunner's pill box. Joe released the pigeons. He and Jeff watched as the gunner shot one pigeon down, but the other flew towards the back lines. Within a few hours, artillery shells rained down on the German machine gun and silenced it.

I never thought I'd be thanking the devil himself for saving my men, Joe mused.

"Jeff, I want you to take Lucifer back to his master in the back lines." Joe said as he scratched the greyhound behind the ears. Joe thought if Jeff got away from the front lines for a while, he may be less anxious and panicked. Joe knew animals always helped.

"Yes, sir, Sergeant Moon," Jeff replied as he took the greyhound by the collar. "Maybe if I get to the back lines, I can have a cigarette. I've been dying for a cigarette."

"You do that, Jeff. Smoke one for me," Joe said. He patted Jeff on the shoulder as he sent him off with the hound.

All the men knew that Joe had been a baseball player before this war. The promise of playing for the troops had never materialized for him. He faced combat every day. And at night he drank; which he had never done before.

A few weeks later, Joe saw Johnny leaning against the wall in the trenches again. Joe couldn't help himself from running up to Johnny and hugging him.

"I saw that you were red-tagged. You should be back at home," Joe said to him.

"I'm not leaving the guys, Sarge. You were so brave to drag me back to the trench. I slipped out of the hospital after they stitched me up. 15 stitches. Lucky for me the Jerry didn't bayonet me in my pitching arm," Johnny smiled.

"I'm happy to have you back," Joe said to his friend. He didn't feel as brave as his friend gave him credit for.

As winter approached, the fighting slowed down. The troops still didn't walk out in the open for fear of being strafed by a German fighter plane. But as the pace of the fighting slowed, it felt like they were making progress. The Germans were pulling back. That only added to the boredom of the soldiers as they waited in the trenches. They sang to each other to pass the time.

Joe took his turn every few weeks going to the rear area for a bath and delousing. He also used the opportunity of being in the rear to drink heavily each night. After one night of heavy boozing he stumbled upon a tent of men sleeping, wrapped in blankets. He was too drunk to get back to his own barracks, so he laid down among them and fell asleep. When he awoke the next morning, he saw a rat peering at him perched atop one of the sleeping men.

"Hey, Buddy," Joe slurred to his sleeping companion. "Wake up." The soldier didn't stir. Joe clumsily rolled over onto his hands and knees. He crawled over to the man to chase the rat away.

"Get out of here," Joe swatted at the rat, and it scurried away. He shook the man, but he didn't move. He was stiff. Joe realized he had fallen asleep among the dead men in a makeshift morgue.

As Joe scrambled to get out of the morgue, he brushed against one of the other bodies and the blanket pulled away from the head. He saw the familiar wiry black hair sticking out. Joe lifted the blanket and saw Jeff's still face, raw with yellow blisters. There was a slight odor of garlic and onions. He must have been gassed when he took the dog back to the rear.

Joe slowly pulled the blanket back up over Jeff's face. Then he fell to his knees in anguish. He had no fight left in him.

When he regained his senses, he staggered outside and poured the whiskey from his flask into the mud. He dumped the bottle into the trash can and swore to himself that he would never drink again. He trudged to the camp canteen to sober up with a cup of coffee and to see if he had any mail from home.

"Harris," a corpsman called out to him. "You have a package."

Joe hurried over to pick up the brown paper-wrapped box from home. He fought back tears when he opened it to find a warm pair of wool socks from his mother and a deck of cards and a letter from his sister, Margaret. As he read the letter, he was reassured that everyone at home still remembered and loved him.

Chapter Ten

Late 1918

After several months of fighting in the Argonne Forest, Joe had seen a lot of dead soldiers and a lot of wounded ones. But if you asked any of the French citizens what had brought the fighting to an end, they would say, "Les Americains."

In November, Joe got into an auto ambulance with seven other men to head for an embarkation camp to go back home. The ambulance was a green Model-T Ford painted with a large red cross on the back. Officially only four seated soldiers were supposed to ride in the back of the ambulance, but they squeezed in twice that number because they all wanted to get back to camp as quickly as they could. They were laughing and joking with each other because the armistice had been signed and the war was over.

The road was narrow and full of holes. Some holes had recently been filled with a few stones. On both sides of the roads were tree stumps and cut up branches to make the Germans think there was no road there. Even though the armistice had been signed, the drivers still were in the habit of not using their lights for fear of being seen from above. The driver was going a little too fast around a curve, and the ambulance overturned into a ditch. All Joe heard was the blasting, shattering crash.

Joe was the most seriously injured, knocked unconscious with a deep laceration near his left eye. When he woke up, he was in a hospital bed surrounded by other injured men. There were rows of iron beds as far as he could see. His head was completely bandaged with his left eye covered. His jaw was wired shut. It hurt to breathe. He tried to move his legs, but they were painful.

In the ward, a nurse in a floor-length blue gown with a white apron noticed he was awake and came to check on him. She had a red cross on the bib of her apron and was wearing a white surgical mask over the lower part of her face.

"Bonjour, Monsieur. Je vois que tu es reveille," she said as she picked up his chart from the foot of the bed. The sunlight from the window behind her made her white nurse's hat look like a halo.

"I don't speak French," Joe said through parched lips that barely opened through the wire around his jaw.

She quickly switched to English. "I see you are awake, Monsieur. How are you feeling?"

"What happened to me? I feel like I got hit by a truck. All that I remember is riding in the ambulance, heading for home. Everything hurts." Joe said.

"The ambulance you were riding in turned over. You have a skull fracture, a broken jaw, a cut below your eye, three broken ribs, and your legs are severely bruised. If you feel the need to swear, Monsieur, I have heard the other men do it and it can help you bear the pain."

"Where am I?" Joe asked her.

"This is a military hospital in Tonnere," she said as she touched his arm. "The doctor will come around later today to check on you. But we are happy that you are awake."

"I can't believe I made it through fighting the Jerrys with hardly a scratch, and on my way home I get hurt in an accident," Joe said with a painful smile.

"At least you are alive, Monsieur," the nurse said, "Many were not so fortunate."

That night Joe listened to the moans from the surrounding beds. He realized that he was one of the lucky ones. But with his eye injured and his legs throbbing, he wondered if he would ever play baseball again. He thought about his friend, Johnny, getting bayonetted. Johnny got 15 stitches and went back to fight again. He thought about Jeff. They had all been through so much.

A few weeks later, Joe took a deep breath, swung his legs over the side of the bed and tried to stand up. The bruising on his legs had turned yellowish green—no longer the deep purple color. The cut on his left eye had partially healed. Because part of his jaw was fractured, and the doctors had to remove 8 pieces of bone from there, it left a huge scar underneath his eye, running from his eye to his chin. Joe grimaced, but he managed to stand. Joe had been assigned a reconstruction aide, and she worked with him to stand and walk a few paces every day. He was determined to be home for Christmas.

The reconstruction aide put Joe in a shower and shot his back and the backs of his legs with a powerful jet of water from a hose. She started with warm water, then raised it to hot, and finished with cold. This lasted for only a minute or two and was supposed to increase his circulation. Joe had to admit he felt better after the treatments.

Joe was shipped to Parkview Hospital in Pittsburgh to finish his recuperation and physical therapy. Joe didn't realize until he arrived that Parkview had not only soldiers returning from the war but also patients who had contracted the Spanish flu. All the doctors and nurses, as well as the patients, wore gauze face masks. Joe was very uncomfortable with the face mask rubbing on his scarred face. But when he saw the orderlies moving bodies out of the ward, at least one every hour, he kept the mask on.

Joe overheard one of the doctors talking to one of the nurses about the flu. "The attack of this disease is almost always sudden. It begins with a chill, severe headache, pain in the back, general tiredness, flushed face, a soreness in the throat, and a fever from 101 to 104 degrees. If you have someone with these symptoms, you are to have them gargle with one teaspoon of salt and one teaspoon of baking soda in a glass of water."

Joe thought to himself, I can't get the flu on top of everything else. Every morning he would take a deep breath for ten seconds and hold it. He thought if he could do that without coughing, that would mean another day without the flu.

When Joe returned to his bed from his therapy sessions, he was able to read the daily newspaper. With sadness, he read that one of the most famous umpires, Silk O'Loughlan, had succumbed to pneumonia from the flu in Boston. Silk had been the umpire in many games that Joe played in. He was only 46 years old. Joe remembered his gestures and peculiar language behind the plate, his long drawn-out 'S-T-R-I-K-E!' and his witty 'Foul-der!' Joe fondly recalled some of their arguments around the bases. Silk was not the only casualty of the flu—many thousands died every day.

The paper had a eulogy from one of O'Loughlan's fellow umpires, Billy Evans. It read: "In the death of Silk O'Loughlan, the country has lost a worthwhile citizen, baseball has lost a remarkable character, and I have lost one of my dearest friends. If there ever was an umpire who gave the plays as he saw them, O'Loughlan was that individual. He had a heart of oak, a keen intellect, and the courage to do what he believed was right, regardless of the opinion of others. He gave the best he had. He never shirked. He never grumbled over an assignment, always accepting them as they came, as part of the game."

Joe harkened back to Silk saying to him, "I have never made a wrong decision. At least if I did, I never admitted it, which amounts to the same thing." Joe remembered a few times when he thought Silk made a wrong decision. Joe tried to grin at the thought, and it hurt his face where the scar was slowly healing. Some days Joe was okay. Some days when he heard about his friends dying from this flu, he was scared.

Doctors were at a loss as to what to recommend for their patients to keep them from getting the flu. They wanted to keep people isolated, but it was difficult with hospital wards overflowing with injured men returning from the war. They recommended eating cinnamon, eating peppers, drinking wine, and drinking Oxo's meat juice, a type of bone broth. No one came to visit Joe in the hospital. He felt a constant, sick panicky feeling at the pit of his stomach. This was a situation he had no control over.

Bodies piled up to such an extent that cemeteries were overwhelmed, and families had to dig graves for their relatives by themselves.

For most people, returning from war was a blessing, but for Joe it was a nightmare. His friends who had returned were happy to see their families again. Joe worried that he would be taking the flu to his family. He also felt a hole in his heart for his men who would never see their families again. He felt responsible because he was the one who ordered them out of the relative safety of the trenches, ordered them to take that machine gun nest, and ultimately ordered them to their deaths.

Finally, the day came in mid-December when Joe was released from the hospital and arrived back in Coulters. He was fortunate to be out of the hospital. The flu had been tough on the mining community because they had few doctors, but luckily none of Joe's family had gotten the flu. Joe hadn't seen them in years, first with all the traveling he did for baseball and then for the war. He would have been devastated if one of them died from the flu while he was gone. He needed no more guilt.

When he walked into the door of the house and stamped the snow off his boots, the whole family was there to greet him. Joe was still wearing his brown wool service coat. Enoch, John, Alexander, William, James, and Thomas all gathered around him hugging him and slapping him on the back. Joe leaned on his cane in order to keep his balance.

"Go easy," Joe said, as he still wasn't as strong as he had been before the war. But he laughed along with them as they pushed and shoved each other like the brothers had always done.

Joe stepped away from his brothers and shook his dad's hand. "I'm proud of you, son."

"Thanks, Pop," Joe said.

His sister Mary and her two children, Neath and Thelma, were standing next to his mother by the Christmas tree. Many of the branches held candle cups with small white candles. And there was a small star on the top. Joe gazed at the star as he hugged his mother, and she had tears rolling down her cheeks. Joe could count on one hand the number of times he had seen his mother cry. She was a stoic woman. But Joe was one of her youngest children and the only one to go so far from home.

"I'm so glad you're home, Joe, and in time for Christmas," his mother said as she wiped away the tears. "So many boys didn't make it back." She distractedly rearranged the stockings on the fireplace mantel that held oranges and nuts for everyone in the family.

"I know, Mum," Joe said. He swiftly ran his hands up and down her arms as if he was warming her.

"Let's all sit down to dinner, now," Annie said. They had pushed two large tables together. "Thelma, you can say grace."

They all held hands around the table as Mary's daughter Thelma spoke. "God is great. God is good. Let us thank Him for our food. By his hands, we are fed. Give us, Lord, our daily bread. Amen."

"Amen," they all chorused.

Joe looked around the table at his cherished family and said, "I lost a few good friends, but we have so much to be thankful for. So, I want to put all that behind me. I want to get back to baseball as soon as the season starts up.

Chapter Eleven

1919

In the spring, Joe had recuperated enough to head back to Cleveland. He still had some trouble walking, and his vision in his left eye was not as good as it was before the war. He had persistent boils on the bottom of one foot, and he couldn't run to field balls as well as he could before the war.

Joe was happy to get back to the team. Lee Fohl was still the manager and wanted to run away with the pennant now that he had some of his best players back from overseas. He shook Joe's hand when he entered the locker room. Joe missed the smell of the old wood cubbies. He wanted just to sit on one of the wooden stools and feel his old life again.

"Glad to have you back, Moon," Fohl said. "I've been reading about you in the *Cleveland Plain Dealer*. After your accident, I wasn't sure you'd be back."

"It wasn't easy over there, but I'll be OK," Joe said. "I guess God was with me."

When Joe first got up to bat, though, he noticed he had to change his stance to see the ball. The scar tissue around his eye blocked what he could see. He crouched and turned his head slightly.

In a July game against the Boston Red Sox, Joe got a chance
to show what he could do despite his eye. He pinch hit a triple
with three on base to give Cleveland a 7 to 3 lead in the last of
the eighth inning. Joe was feeling good about this game, but
then relief pitcher Elmer Myers gave up a run. Then he loaded
the bases on walks.

Tris Speaker was still a big part of the Cleveland team as an
outfielder but also as Lee Fohl's right-hand man. From the outfield, he signaled to Fohl that another relief pitcher should come
in. Fohl didn't quite understand Speaker's signal, so he put in
their little used left-handed pitcher, Fritz Coumbe. Speaker
didn't want to appear that he was overruling his manager—but
he didn't want Coumbe to pitch to the next Red Sox batter.

The next Red Sox batter was Babe Ruth. At 6' 2" and over
200 pounds, Ruth stepped up to the plate and hit his second
home run of the day to give the Red Sox an 8 to 7 win.

As soon as the game was over, Indians owner Jack Dunn
called Fohl into his office.

"Fohl, what were you thinking putting a southpaw up
against Babe Ruth? You're fired!" Dunn said. Lee Fohl was
one of the youngest managers Dunn had ever hired. He had believed in him up until this point. Dunn moved Tris Speaker up
to manage the Tribe in Fohl's place.

Joe caught up with Fohl as he was leaving the ballpark. Joe
walked with him down the long corridor. He put his arm on his
friend's shoulder.

"You got a raw deal, Lee." Joe said. "Why didn't you tell
Dunn that it was Speaker's idea to pitch Coumbe?"

"You been in charge of men in the war. You know it's always the fault of the man in charge, Moon," Fohl said. "And

what about that Babe Ruth? He's really something, isn't he? I would love to manage the team that he is on."

"Yeah, he's OK," Joe said. "I'd like to go up against him to hit a few of his pitches. I could take him down a few notches."

Joe played 62 games for Cleveland, but he wasn't satisfied with how he was playing. He continued to get better despite his war injuries, but Speaker wasn't playing him as much as Fohl did.

Fall arrived, and the players from Cleveland already knew they had clinched second place in their league. On September 24th they had a game in Detroit against the Tigers at "The Corner," as Navin Field was known. Detroit was in fourth place in the league. Detroit beat Cleveland 4 to 1 at that game, and the Cleveland players intended to break training and party into the evening. Cleveland would not be prepared to battle Detroit at their game the following day on September 25th at full strength.

"Come on with you, Joe," Steve O'Neill said. "This is my part of town, and we're heading out to the Nancy Whiskey Pub." The Detroit ballpark was in a part of town called Corktown. It had been settled by Irish immigrants who came from County Cork.

"I'm coming, Steve," Joe said as he finished tying his tie.

"I want you to be having a proper shot of Tullemore Dew," Steve said. "It's on me, so it is." Joe thought he had taken his last shot of whiskey when he was in France. But he craved the numb feeling it gave him. Steve drank heavily ever since he came back from the war and Joe liked to join him.

"And how about you, Smoky," Steve asked Indians pitcher Joe Wood who was nicknamed Smoky Joe. "Will you be joinin' us at the pub?"

"You go along without me. I'm meeting up with Tris and a couple of the Tigers tonight," Smoky said.

After the game, Smoky met underneath the grandstands with Tris Speaker; Dutch Leonard, pitcher for the Tigers; and Ty Cobb, manager of the Tigers.

Ty Cobb introduced them to Fred West. West was particularly tall and kept looking back over his shoulder when he was introduced. "Tris, Smoky, this here's Fred West. He works here at Navin. He'll be taking our bets. How much do you want to put up?"

"$1,000 from each of us for the Tigers to win," Tris spoke for Smoky and himself. He pulled an envelope from his suit coat pocket. He thought the envelope made it more discreet.

Ty Cobb was counting out $2,000 in hundreds to hand to West. Dutch Leonard had $1,500. They were both out in the open about handing the money to the shifty bookie.

"We don't want anyone to know we're doing this," Tris said.

"Mums the word," West said with an obnoxious wink.

If Detroit beat Cleveland, the Tigers could come in third place in the American League over the New York Yankees. It would get each of their players an additional $500 for the season.

Smoky took Speaker aside and whispered, "Tris, you know the guys have all headed out to the Irish pub. They're goin' to be partyin' all night."

Speaker turned away from Smoky and said to Leonard and Cobb, "The Tigers don't have to worry about tomorrow's game. We've got second place cinched and you will win tomorrow."

"Don't you feel the least bit bad that you're betting against your own team?" Cobb asked him.

"I don't feel like I'm betting against my own team. I feel like I'm betting against the Yankees coming into third place in the league. And I don't want Ruth to get that extra $500 after what he did to Fohl."

"Do you think Babe Ruth cares about an extra $500?" Cobb huffed.

On that cold and raw day in Detroit, the Tigers won the game 9 to 5. "The Corner" had a dark blue hitter's backdrop in center field, and Joe used it when he got up to bat. Joe got one double and spent most of his time fielding ground balls before the batters even got to first base. It was tough to keep up the pace because he had been out so late and only slept for a few fitful hours. His head was splitting from a hangover. And every bone broken in the ambulance accident ached from the cold.

Joe saw Smoky talking to West in the locker room after the game. He overheard West mumble, "Detroit was the local favorite. Heavily favored to win. The bookies would only handle so much money."

"Look, I could only put down $600, with none of it belonging to Cobb or Speaker. Each of you only gets $420," West continued.

"We each gave you $1000, and we get back $420?" Smoky questioned.

"That's the way it goes," West said as he smiled around the stub of a cigar.

Joe saw Smoky Wood roll up his stack of hundreds and put it into his pocket. "Where d'you come by that big stack of cash?" Joe walked over and asked him when West left.

"You know we bet on the game. Me and Speaker," Smoky said. Joe knew that players occasionally bet on the games.

"How could you do that?" Joe asked as he shook his head disgustedly. "To bet that your own team would lose."

Smoky said, "It didn't matter in the end for the standings. You know what else? Cobb bet on his team to win but did not get up one cent. If we do this again, we know we have to try to get down early."

"Just stop. Just stop speaking," Joe said. Joe rubbed his whisker-studded chin with his hand.

"Don't go acting like you're so much better than me. You and O'Neill were so hungover you could barely play."

Joe questioned the idea that the game was thrown because neither Leonard nor Wood played in the game. Cobb, on the winning side, managed only a single in five at-bats. Speaker had three hits, including two triples. It didn't seem like Speaker would hit like that if he was trying to throw the game. Joe and Steve had played their best, but they were both hungover. Despite that, Joe was still very upset with Speaker because his friend, Lee Fohl, had just been fired and Speaker had taken his place. Fohl would never sell out his team.

The next week, Joe received two letters. One was a contract offer from Cleveland for $5,000 for the 1920 season. The other was a letter from L. L. Jacklin, a prominent businessman and the owner of an industrial baseball team in Franklin City, Pennsylvania. Joe had a decision to make.

The letter, printed on satiny, buff-colored paper, read as follows:

Dear Mr. Harris,

The Franklin Millionaires baseball team would like to offer you a position as a first baseman with the team. Our *scouts have been watching you play with Cleveland and are impressed with your statistics. The starting date would be immediate, and the salary would be $5,000 per year paid on a weekly basis.*

If you choose to accept this offer, please sign the second copy of this letter and return it to me immediately. When your acknowledgment is received, we will send a bus ticket to you for the trip to Franklin.

We look forward to welcoming you to the Franklin Millionaires team.

Sincerely,

L. L. Jacklin

Glass Snappers National Protective Association of America President

Owner, Franklin Millionaires Baseball Team

After learning that one of his teammates and his manager bet against their own team, Joe returned the contract to Cleveland unsigned and headed to Franklin to talk to Mr. Jacklin in person about playing in an "outlaw" league.

Chapter Twelve

1920

Joe arrived at the Glass Snappers National Protective Association of America building in Franklin, Pennsylvania, on a warm spring day. A secretary showed him into the office of Mr. Jacklin, who stood up from behind an imposing dark brown desk to greet him.

"How great to finally meet the Moon," Mr. Jacklin gushed as he shook Joe's hand. "And I hear you're a war hero, too."

"Thank you, Mr. Jacklin," Joe said as he glanced around the plush room. "Every time I've talked about the war, the story gets exaggerated, so I've cut out talking about it."

"Let's get right down to business," Jacklin said. "We want you to come and play for the Franklin Millionaires. The Franklin people would love to have a real war hero on their town team. And we need you to beat our rivals, the Oil City Independents."

Joe had done a little homework before this trip. The Franklin team was part of the Two Team League with Oil City, Pennsylvania. Originally both Franklin and Oil City were part of a bigger circuit known as the Interstate League. But the Interstate League had lost a lot of money in the past few years and had dwindled to only two teams. The teams continued to play one another and held a few exhibition games every year. They played against company teams from Western Pennsylvania, the New Kensington Aluminums and the Elk County Elcos. They also played against the Pittsburgh Collegians, a team comprising college players who played in the summers. If Joe signed on with the Franklin team, he would play outlaw baseball. The outlaw leagues were not linked to the American League of organized baseball. Playing in this league would be a risk for him if it did not work out.

"Mr. Jacklin, I appreciate your offer," Joe said. "But the Cleveland team already offered me $5,000 to play with them this year. So, I would need more than that to come and play for Franklin."

"Well, I don't think I can offer you more money this year," Jacklin said, emphasizing the word 'money.' "The last few years have been tough on the league. I'm sure you know that. The weather has been tough on us. But I want you to meet two friends of mine at lunch. I think we have an offer that will interest you."

Joe looked around at the paintings and sculptures in the swanky room and thought for sure that Mr. Jacklin could better the Cleveland offer.

Joe and Mr. Jacklin walked down 12th Street and turned the corner onto Liberty Street. They soon stepped into the lobby of the Commercial Hotel. There were two men waiting for them. Both men wore fine dark suits.

"Joe, this is Mr. Homer D. Biery and Mr. Lawrence D. Gent, proprietors of this beautiful hotel," Jacklin said.

"Pleased to meet you," Joe said.

"The pleasure is ours," Mr. Gent said. "It's not every day you get to meet a baseball star and a war hero."

"I'm no war hero. I just went to fight the Jerrys like everyone else," Joe said humbly.

"Let's have some lunch," Mr. Gent said as he gently patted Joe on the back.

They entered a big dining room. The Commercial Hotel was not a grand hotel like the ones Joe had seen in Europe. But it was four stories tall and part of the bustling downtown. The dining room had four large crystal chandeliers. All the tables had crisp white tablecloths. There were men and women dressed in business clothes eating lunch throughout. The four men sat down at one of the tables.

"What do you think of this hotel?" Mr. Gent asked.

"It's very nice, sir," Joe said.

"How would you like to own a piece of it?" Mr. Gent asked.

"Oh, I could never afford something like this," Joe exclaimed. "I was just an army sergeant and now I'm getting back to playing baseball. I don't have the kind of money to buy part of a hotel."

"We are thinking about cutting this dining room in half. Making the other half into a billiard room and possibly even putting in a small bowling alley. Franklin is growing, and the men coming back from the war need some amusements. Now understand, with Prohibition just becoming a law this past January, you won't be able to serve the men anything other than soda pop. But if you keep the pool tables rotating, the men won't even miss the alcohol. And who better to run all this than our very own baseball hero." Mr. Gent said.

"You come to play for Franklin. Take care of the billiard room on your off days and in the winter," Mr. Biery added.

Joe glanced over at Mr. Jacklin, who was just sitting at the table smiling at him. "We will do all the promotion for you, Joe."

Joe didn't know what to say. This was quite an offer. He could still play baseball, and they would set him up in a business at only 29 years old. But he had done nothing like this before.

"May I take the night to think about it?" Joe asked.

"Let us know your answer in the morning," Jacklin said.

In the morning, Joe was prepared to give them his answer. Even though the Cleveland Indians seemed like they were headed to the World Series and Joe would have loved to be a part of a winning team, Joe thought he would take on the billiard room at the Commercial Hotel. He thought about his injuries sustained in the war and knew he was slowing down. Maybe he wouldn't be able to keep up with the Cleveland team and would cost them the World Series. He didn't want to do that to his teammates. He thought about the cheating scandal last year and how that disgusted him. If he got the billiard parlour, even his friends from the war could come and visit with him during the off season. Billiards was relatively new. If he could learn how to lead men into battle, he could learn the billiards business.

Joe walked back over to Jacklin's office in the morning. "Before you say anything," Mr. Jacklin said, "my business partners, and I talked last night, and you were right. The offer is too low and doesn't beat Cleveland's offer hands down, like we wanted to do. So, we will throw in an apartment upstairs at the hotel along with the billiard parlor."

Joe could hardly believe this. Now the offer was really too good to pass on. He kept repeating over and over in his head, *I will still play baseball, too.*

"You've got a deal," Joe enthusiastically thrust out his hand. He pumped Mr. Jacklin's hand hard a couple of times.

Joe installed 6 billiard tables in a walled off section of the dining room and 10 bowling alley lanes in the hotel's basement. The basement had soundproofing, good lighting, and even air conditioning. His billiards and bowling alleys were the place to be for young men, and all of his baseball friends gathered there. Many veterans returning from the war came to play. Joe used the time when renovating the hotel to dry out from his drinking. He realized he had to stop after the betting scandal. Smoky was right to call him out on his drinking. He had to set an example for his new teammates here in Franklin.

After several weeks, Joe put up a sign at the entrance to the billiard hall. The new name of the "Grand Billiard Parlour" went at the top, and "Ladies Invited" went below that. He thought having a few ladies around might bring in more customers. Because he wasn't serving alcohol, he thought women would feel comfortable there.

It surprised him when a tall, blue-eyed brunette with big dimples on each cheek walked into the parlour for the first time. She was wearing a mauve, vertically striped dress, low at the waist, with a grey cloche felt hat. Some small pearl earrings peeked out from under the hat. The mauve in the dress made her skin glow. Joe thought she was jaw-dropping beautiful.

"I just wanted to check out the new place in town," she said when she noticed Joe standing directly inside the doorway.

"I'm Joe Harris, the owner," he introduced himself. "Let me show you around." He was happy that his voice didn't crack.

"Pleased to meet you, Mr. Harris. I'm Pearl Hepner," she replied and tilted her head. She held out her gloved hand for Joe to shake. "I work at the telephone company across the street and noticed the new sign. I thought I would come over on my lunch hour. Everyone in town has heard of Joe the Moon Harris."

Joe blushed immediately. His heart felt like it was beating out of his chest, but he tried to stay relaxed. Pearl threaded her arm through his outstretched elbow. He walked her through the poolroom like they were walking on the deck of a cruise ship. He had never been around a woman so winsome and glamourous.

"What do you do at the telephone company?" Joe asked.

"I work the switchboard. It's a lot more complicated than most people think," Pearl replied.

Men in suits were shooting billiards, and a few were shooting the new 9-ball game on the green felt-covered tables. "It all looks so fresh and new," Pearl exclaimed as she picked up a piece of blue chalk from the edge of one of the tables.

"We only opened a few weeks ago, so it is new," Joe said. "Now, let me take you downstairs and show you the bowling alley."

Pearl could hear the balls crashing into the pins as she cautiously descended the stairs in her black pumps. Joe stepped slowly behind her. More men dressed in dark tweed suits were bowling.

"Can I get you a soda?" Joe asked.

"Oh, no thanks, I've got to get back to work. But this is just lovely, Joe," she said. "I've lived in Franklin all my life, and we've had nothing like this. Thank you for the tour. I'll be on my way now, but I'll tell all my friends about this place. I think you need a few more ladies in here to liven it up a little."

Joe watched Pearl walk back up the steps and out of the bowling alley. He hoped she would turn back to wave at him, but that didn't happen. Now he would just have to wait to see if she returned.

Summer passed with Joe playing ball for the Franklin Millionaires. He became more and more popular. He was in the local newspaper almost every day in articles written by Jim Borland. His baseball teammates brought all of their friends to the billiard parlour after the games. Joe's friend Steve O'Neill, who was still a catcher for the Indians, loved to bowl, and he was at the bowling alley every week when he could get away from Cleveland. Joe hoped that Pearl would walk through the doors after one of his games or that he would see her in the stands, but that didn't happen. When he thought of her, he could almost hear the sound of her laughter.

Throughout the month of September, Franklin and Oil City met in a twelve-game post-season contest. They played six games in each city because the fans were clamoring for it. The board decided to keep admission prices at 50 cents per game with a 15 cents addition for sitting in the grandstands. But as the games started, Joe was crippled and on crutches with blistery boils on his feet. Without the crutches, he was unable to walk. It was a trench foot condition left over from the war when his feet were continually wet. He had persistent itching and tingling in his feet, and they felt cold and heavy when he tried to walk. Exactly when his services with the team were needed the most, Joe had to let down his fans.

Joe was leaning on his crutches outside the billiard parlour door lighting a cigarette when Jake Pitler walked past him out onto the street. Jake had played with Joe on the Chattanooga team and was now the second baseman for the Oil City team.

"What ya' know, Jake," Joe said as he balanced on one crutch to shake Jake's hand.

"How's tricks, Moon," Jake acknowledged. Joe and Jake were about the same height so they could look each other in the eye now that they were playing on opposing teams.

"What are you doing in Franklin? Shouldn't you be in Oil City relishing your victory?" Joe asked.

"I have a date with a pretty little thing who works right across the street," Jake said. "She's a real blue serge. I'm going to take her out for lunch today."

Joe leaned on the doorjamb and watched through a cloud of cigarette smoke as Pearl walked out of the phone company door and took Jake's arm. They walked off down the street towards the café. Joe felt his stomach sink and a catch in his throat.

At Christmas time, Joe decided to sell Christmas trees on the sidewalk outside of the Grand Billiard Parlour. He sold both pine and cedar trees that he brought in by wagon from a farm outside of town. He decorated the windows of the parlour with colorful lights made by General Electric's new Edison division. The town decorated Liberty Street with lights and skyline wreath garlands at each block. The hardware store had a wooden sign decorated with tinsel that read, "Get the boy something he wants," with two bicycles suspended from wires. The toy store had rows and rows of dolls under a tree decorated with baby carriages. Franklin was looking very festive for the holidays.

Joe was standing outside brushing the snow off a few of the trees when someone tapped him on the shoulder. He turned around to find Pearl standing there with an older gentleman.

She was wearing a thick fur coat that wrapped close to her face. It made her blue eyes sparkle.

"Pearl," Joe exclaimed. He felt trembling butterflies in his stomach. He thought he would never see her again.

"I didn't know if you would remember me or not," Pearl said. Joe thought to himself, he could barely think of anything else since the day she had entered the billiard hall.

"I remember you," Joe said.

"This is my father, Billy Hepner," Pearl introduced the tall, older man standing next to her.

"It's a pleasure to meet the famous Joe Harris," Billy said as they shook hands.

"It's a pleasure to meet you, too, Mr. Hepner. I try to not let all that famous stuff go to my head." Joe asked. "What brings you to Franklin?"

"We're looking to buy a Christmas tree, and my little girl here said this was the only place to buy one. And please, call me Billy," he said.

"I'm flattered," Joe said. "I think there are many places to buy Christmas trees."

"She may have had an ulterior motive," Billy said with a wink.

"Daddy," Pearl exclaimed with a playful swat to her father's arm.

Joe blushed again, and he hoped that Pearl's father thought he was just red-cheeked from the cold.

"Let's go inside and warm up with a cup of coffee," Joe said. "I'll have one of the guys here load the best tree on the lot onto your car."

After the coffee, Pearl's father went outside to see if the tree was strapped to his car. This left Joe and Pearl a little time

alone. Joe had to ask her about Jake Pitler. He had to know what
was going on.

"I'd like to see you again," Joe said quietly as he leaned in
a little towards Pearl so no one else would hear him, "but I saw
you a couple of weeks ago on the arm of Jake Pitler. Are you
dating him?"

Joe didn't want to tell Pearl the whole story. He didn't want
to tell her that he knew Jake in Chattanooga and thought he was
a hot head. Joe and Jake had gotten into arguments over trivial
things like picking up the wrong bat or who would go out the
door first when they left the stadium. When he saw her walking
down the street with him, he wanted to tell her she wouldn't be
happy with him. He wanted to tell her to listen to him and go
out with him instead.

Pearl laughed. "I did go out to lunch with Jake once. But we
didn't hit it off. I'll let you in on a little secret, I was hoping
you would see us and get jealous. I didn't want to go out with
him again."

Joe heaved a sigh of relief. "May I take you out next week?"

"I think that would be wonderful," Pearl replied.

On the next weekend, Joe picked up Pearl for their date. Joe
loved looking at Pearl. She painted her lips a bright red that set
off her hair and eyes. "Do you have some ice skates?" Joe asked
when he arrived at the door with his skates in hand.

"Of course, I do. Let me get them," Pearl replied.

They walked across the 13th Street Bridge and went to the
island in the middle of French Creek. People had set up some
torches along the creek and skimmed the snow from the frozen
river. There were already lines scored all over the ice, like a
giant monk had been practicing his calligraphy there with
swirls and curlicues.

Joe and Pearl laughed as they sat on a bench to put on their skates. Joe never felt so at ease with another person. Fortunately, Pearl had heavy tights on under her knee-length skirt, so she wasn't too cold. Soon she and Joe were gliding around the makeshift rink. Pearl hit a little bump in the ice that almost caused her to fall down, but Joe caught her. Then he kissed her. He had never kissed a woman before. He felt the same nervous flutter that he felt the first time he saw her.

"Pearl, I know we don't know each other very well, but do you believe in love at first sight?" Joe asked her. "Because I'm in love with you. I knew I loved you the first time I saw you."

Pearl looked into Joe's blue eyes, smiled, and ran her gloved hand over the side of Joe's face. Joe turned his head away from her because that was the side of his face disfigured in the war.

"I never felt this way about a man before. I'm in love with you, too," Pearl replied as she pulled his scarred face close to hers and kissed him again.

Luckily Joe wasn't playing ball in the winter and had time to court his new girlfriend. He took her out to dinner once a week. Even though there was snow on the ground, they took long walks around Franklin. He held her hand as they walked across the bridge from the main part of town to the ballpark. He couldn't believe someone as beautiful and sophisticated as Pearl was interested in someone like him, a country boy from Coulters, Pennsylvania.

Chapter Thirteen

1921

Joe had a crazy idea for starting 1921 off. He bought a huge banner made of newsprint with the December calendar month printed on it. It covered the whole front of the billiard parlour. He got the huge piece of newsprint from Pearl's father, who ran the Rocky Grove newspaper. At midnight, he would have a beautiful woman break through the banner to enter the new year. And he had just the person for the job, his girlfriend Pearl. Pearl laughed at the idea, but she said she would do it.

"10, 9, 8," they all counted down as it got close to midnight. "3, 2, 1, Happy New Year!" and Pearl tore through the paper with her arms scissoring like she was swimming through a pool of deep water. The crowd whistled, cheered, and blew horns.

But that wasn't the only surprise up Joe's sleeve. After she broke through the paper and everyone applauded, Joe got down on one knee in front of her. He held out a baseball that he had cut in half and inserted a diamond ring in it, "Pearl Hepner, will you spend the rest of your life with me hitting it out of the park? Will you marry me?"

"Yes, yes, 1,000 times, yes!" Pearl said.

Joe broke out some sparkling cider and poured glasses for all of his friends.

Joe married Pearl on February 4th in Meadville, Pennsylvania. Joe's mother came with his brother, Thomas, but his other siblings couldn't make it. Pearl's parents were there with her brothers, Les and Francis. Reverend Mr. Walker married them in the First Baptist Church, a white clapboard church with a simple steeple. Pearl wore an ivory white tea length dress of satin with a floor-length embroidered veil. The veil had a headband decorated with pearls, and she had a long strand of pearls around her neck. She wore bright red lipstick because she knew that Joe liked it. Joe didn't think anyone looked more beautiful than his bride. He smiled from ear to ear as he watched her walk down the aisle of the church.

At the end of the ceremony, Reverend Mr. Walker said, "I now pronounce you, man and wife. You may kiss the bride."

Joe lifted Pearl's veil and kissed her for a long time on the lips. "I love you," he whispered into her ear before they turned to face their guests.

The wedding party pulled up in their horse-drawn carriage to the portico in front of the grand Lafayette Hotel and quickly ran inside to dodge the cold raindrops. Their family and friends waited for them at the reception. Joe was hoping to arrive with Pearl in a horse-drawn sleigh but there was no snow, only rain. He wanted everyone to look at her as his princess.

Joe feasted his eyes on Pearl as she cut into their white sponge wedding cake decorated with white feathers and topped with a white flower. She glowed in the low light of the hotel ballroom, and everyone else in the room faded away. He was floating on air.

Pearl wrote in her little white wedding diary in big, loopy cursive writing. "This certifies that Joseph Harris and Pearl Julia Hepner were united in Holy Matrimony on the 4th day of February A.D. 1921 according to the rights of the Baptist Church and the laws of the state of Pennsylvania."

Joe and Pearl went on a wedding trip to Youngstown, Cleveland, and Pittsburgh for the rest of the month of February. Pearl was secretly hoping to go to Niagara Falls, but she knew that Joe had to conduct business while on the trip. She had to settle for a trip to Lanterman's Mill in Youngstown, Ohio, a mill next to a beautiful, natural waterfall. The mill building held a ballroom and a concession stand. Joe and Pearl danced there each night for a week, looking out the windows at the frozen waterfall.

As Pearl fell asleep beside Joe in bed for the first time, he laid awake and looked at her. One of her hands rested delicately against her throat, like a bee alighting on a flower, as she laid on her back. He listened to her light breathing as her chest rose and fell under the blankets. He could see a sliver of a crescent moon through the window. He snuggled up against her while trying not to wake her. He gently kissed her cheek. Then he, too, fell asleep.

"Good morning, Mrs. Harris," Joe said to Pearl when she awoke. Pearl smiled and kissed him.

"It's the start of many good mornings together, Mr. Harris," Pearl replied. As they laid next to each other in bed, Pearl reached over to grasp and massage Joe's earlobe between her finger and thumb. Joe closed his eyes and let out a deep sigh. Pearl didn't seem to mind his broken body. Just the opposite. He never believed he could be this happy.

Joe's thoughts returned to baseball in the spring. He was playing for the Franklin Millionaires, but in his heart he wanted to return to organized baseball. When Joe joined the Franklin team, he had received a letter from Baseball Commissioner Kenesaw Mountain Landis banning him from baseball for life. The exact words in the letter said that Joe had "played with and against ineligible players in independent games." Joe knew when he went to play for the outlaw league that he was taking a chance that he would never return to organized baseball.

On a rainy Monday in May, Joe was playing checkers with the other players in the Miller-Sibley field clubhouse before their opening day practice. The manager of the Millionaires, John Brackenridge, introduced the players to an elderly newspaper reporter, Jim Borland. With thin, white hair, wire-rimmed glasses, and a loose-fitting suit, Jim looked more like the country doctor than a sports reporter. His back had a small hump, so it looked like he was hunched over his notebook even though he wasn't.

Joe reached out to shake Jim's hand. "I've been reading the 'Jim Borland's Column' in the News-Herald since I moved here," Joe said. "I enjoy your nature writing. I do a lot of hunting in the off season. I like walking around in the woods just as much as I do hunting game."

"The older I get, the more I enjoy being out in nature," Jim said. "But today, I need to write a full page spread on this year's Franklin team. So, let's start with you. Are you married?"

"Yes, just got married a few months ago to a beautiful Franklin gal," Joe said.

"And where did you play before?" Jim asked.

"I played in the American League and in the Southern Michigan League," Joe said.

"So, you've been around. Where do you call home?" Jim asked.

"I grew up in Coulters. I just moved to Franklin a year or so ago. I own the Grand Billiard Parlour," Joe said proudly.

Jim scratched some notes into his notebook as Joe talked. "Thank you, Mr. Harris," Jim said as he looked up at Joe with friendly blue eyes.

"Mr. Harris is so formal. You can call me 'Moon' like my friends do. Maybe when the season is over, we can get together and do some hunting," Joe said.

The interviews were soon over and the players suited up. They went outside and every player was loaded into an automobile for a parade. The parade left the ball grounds down 13th to Liberty, to 11th, to Elk, to 10th, and back to Liberty to head back to the field. Horns were honking all the way. When they got back to the ball grounds, the Boy Scout band played as they walked onto the field.

The rain stopped but the field was still wet. The mayor threw out the first pitch, and then the Franklin team heard the umpire say, "Play ball."

Joe hit the first home run of the season in the fifth inning. It flew a mile high and landed well outside of the fence with the newly painted advertising signs. The crowd of nearly 2,000 cheered as Joe trotted around the bases. That one home run wasn't enough, though. The two teams battled to a 2 to 2 tie in the tenth inning when the game was called. There wasn't enough daylight to go on.

Despite the great opening, Franklin was having trouble keeping the team afloat. Franklin had to host a Booster Day to raise enough money to pay the players for the 1921 season. Fans were asked to pay $1.50 for a seat rather than their usual

$1.00. Having this Booster Day was the only way they could continue to enjoy baseball in Franklin. The gate receipts were not enough to pay the salaries of all the players. Joe knew this would be a big game, so he planned to put on a show for the fans.

In the first inning, Joe lofted one towards the right field fence and yelled, "Farewell!" into the stands. But the Oil City right outfielder made a running catch, and the inning was over.

Next time up at bat, Joe hit a double. Then he hit the longest home run ever seen at Miller-Sibley Field over the middle field fence. By the end of the game Joe had two home runs, two doubles, and four singles. Franklin beat Oil City 10 to 9. Even the umpires told Joe that he had given the crowd a great game.

When Joe got home that night, he told Pearl, "I played one of the best games of my life tonight, but I'm not sure if I'm pulling in enough fans to keep the team profitable. There just doesn't seem to be enough money."

Pearl took one of his hands in hers and held it to her lips. "You're always so hard on yourself. You're doing the best you can."

Despite his phenomenal batting, Joe's fears were realized in July when the manager, John Brackenridge, called the team together in the clubhouse. "Men, I'm sorry to have to be the one to tell you this. But you're all going to have to take a 25% pay cut so we can finish out this season," Bracky said.

Joe heard groans throughout the dugout. Joe had the billiard parlour and bowling alley to fall back on for income, but many of the players didn't have that luxury.

A week later, Brackenridge took Joe aside. "Listen Joe, the Franklin team is going under for sure. I have a contract for you to play with the Clearfield team, the Terriers. They want me to come and pitch for them. They asked me to get you to come along."

"I hate to leave Franklin for another independent league team, John. If I'm leaving this team, I'd like to go back to Cleveland," Joe said.

"It's the best we have right now. To finish out the season," Bracky said. By the end of the week, the Franklin team had folded.

After playing only eight games with Clearfield, Joe's batting average was an unheard of .471. It didn't seem to matter that the Clearfield fence was much farther away than the one at Miller-Sibley Field—he could still smash a hit over that fence. They paid Joe $100 for each game, but he had a bad feeling about the way things were going with the outlaw leagues. He thought he should try to get back to organized baseball. He wanted to play for Cleveland again. He missed his friends there.

Pearl had the letter in her hand when Joe came in the door from his game in Clearfield. "It's a letter from Boston," she said.

Joe ripped open the letter and read it out loud. "If you can guarantee your reinstatement with the American League, we would like to offer you a trade from Cleveland for a position with the Boston Red Sox."

Pearl frowned. "Do you think they will reinstate you?"

"The only way we'll know is to ask. I'll write a letter to Judge Landis and see what he says," Joe said. "Do you want to move to Boston?"

"I'll follow you anywhere," Pearl said. "But do you think we can keep our home in Franklin, too? Your business is here. And my family is here."

"Franklin will always be our winter home. We can invite all the guys on the old Franklin team to come and see us when they're not playing. It's exciting to be traded to a new team, especially when you know the team values you and wants your services," Joe said.

Joe and Pearl had been following the news in the papers about Judge Landis, possibly black balling Babe Ruth from playing in organized baseball because Babe Ruth went on a barnstorming tour in the off season to play ball in exhibition games. Babe Ruth said it was unAmerican to not let him play in whatever games he wanted to play. But as the commissioner, Judge Landis was trying to bring order to the chaos of baseball.

In December, the Red Sox were in last place. Joe wanted to get to work with them and change their standing in the league with his hitting. But he still had to be reinstated. He was granted a hearing with Judge Landis to be held on February 4th of 1922.

1922

P earl looked at the calendar. "February 4th has to be a good omen! The same day as our wedding anniversary!"

"I've had so many coincidences in my life, Pearl." Joe said. "But I hate to spend our first wedding anniversary in a courtroom begging for my job."

"Well, I'm going to announce it out loud to the universe that it will be our lucky day," Pearl declared.

Joe stopped at the barber shop and had his hair trimmed. He wore his best suit and had his shoes shined. He carried copies of his war record and his old contracts in his briefcase. He wanted to be prepared for anything the Commissioner asked him.

Joe and Pearl traveled to Chicago and were dwarfed by the size of the Chicago Federal Building. The gray granite building had two stair-step stories and was topped by an octagonal dome. They looked up at the dome to see a huge stone eagle perched on each corner.

They entered through the central arch. Once inside, their steps echoed as they crossed the marble tiles and rode up in a wrought iron elevator to the sixth floor. The courtroom had twenty-foot ceilings and skylights to let in natural light. Along the frieze was a huge mural showing former President Abraham Lincoln practicing law.

Despite the grandiose courtroom, Judge Kenesaw Landis still made an imposing figure. With his stark black suit, he seemed a wiry, tense man ready to spring. His clean-shaven face sported a perpetual frown. His dark brown eyes stared sternly ahead. Silvery gray hair swooped down his forehead and almost covered one eye.

Joe stood in front of the judge's bench with his hat in his hands. He rotated the hat nervously around and around to keep his hands busy. The courtroom was so quiet that Joe could hear people breathing all around him.

"My first inclination, Mr. Harris, is to deny your request. You would be the first player to be reinstated, and I want to make sure we set the correct precedence. I am not interested in these rogue players doing whatever they want to do. But I see in your request to be reinstated that you served in the war," Commissioner Landis said.

"Yes, sir. I fought with the 320th in France," Joe replied. He tried to swallow but his mouth was dry.

"And you were injured?" Landis asked.

"Yes, sir. They gassed me frequently. And I was in a bad accident on my way home. I had some injuries to my skull. I busted my jaw in eight places and got this big scar. Several broken ribs. But I haven't let that stop me playing ball. I love baseball, sir."

"Do you still have headaches?" Landis asked.

"Sometimes, sir. And I get a burning feeling in my back and legs that no amount of ice or massaging will help," Joe replied.

"Perhaps the headaches and the gassing in the war caused you to make some poor decisions. Your experiences of being shot at caused you to do things that you might not otherwise have done. I can't imagine the bitter fighting you have seen."

Commissioner Landis paused, and the courtroom got so quiet again that Joe heard his watch ticking. The judge made a steeple with his fingers, pressed his two index fingers to his lips and stared at some papers on his desk. Joe held his breath.

Commissioner Landis continued, "With that said, Mr. Harris, I will reinstate you to play organized baseball with Cleveland in the American League."

Joe heaved a sigh of relief. "Thank you, sir. I won't let you down."

Joe turned back to the gallery in the courtroom. Pearl was waiting for him in the first row. He hugged her, twirling her and lifting her off the ground.

"I told you it would be our lucky day!" Pearl smiled. "Now let's go home."

"Before we go home, we have to celebrate," Joe said.

Joe led Pearl to a bar and pool hall at the corner of Huron and Orleans Streets, markedly named the Huron-Orleans Restaurant. Joe had read about it in the travel guides. This was the only wooden structure to have survived the Great Chicago Fire.

"This is the place for us, Pearl. This green wooden building survived, and so have I, to fight another day," Joe said as they entered under the awning and illuminated name sign. Joe and Pearl walked past the mahogany bar with the large arched mirror to a small table in the back, close to the pool room where they felt at home.

"If we weren't in the middle of Prohibition and if I hadn't sworn off Demon Rum, we'd have champagne to celebrate.

We'll have to settle for some non-alcoholic beer," Joe said. The waiter brought them each a glass.

"To surviving," Pearl said as she clinked her glass against Joe's in a toast and took a sip.

"And let's not forget, happy one-year anniversary to my beautiful wife," Joe said. To celebrate their anniversary, they had a dinner of broiled spring chicken on toast, French peas, potato croquettes, and caramel custard pudding for dessert.

"Happy anniversary. Three hundred and sixty five days just flew by," Pearl said, and they touched glasses together again.

"Paper is the one-year anniversary gift. So, I got this for you," Joe said. He produced a small gift cabinet of Crane's linen stationery from his briefcase. Pearl lifted the cover and found that the creamy paper and envelopes were embossed with her monogram, name, and address.

"Oh, Joe, it's beautiful," she exclaimed. "I won't want to send a letter to anyone. I'll just want to keep it for myself. It's so pretty."

When they returned from Chicago and got back to their apartment in Franklin, Pearl took Joe by the hand. "I have an anniversary surprise for you, too. Close your eyes," she said.

Joe closed his eyes and followed Pearl from the front hallway into the kitchen.

"Open them," Pearl said.

There in the kitchen in a basket on the floor was a small black and white English pointer puppy. Joe knelt down and started petting him. The puppy wiggled and climbed into Joe's lap. He licked Joe's face as Joe scratched his ears. He had one patch of black over one eye and a heart-shaped patch of black on one side.

"He's so sweet, Pearl." Joe smiled. "But a little wild. How did you pull this off? We were in Chicago for days." The puppy made a little woof sound when Joe put him back in the basket.

"I thought you could use something like this no matter how the reinstatement went. If it went wrong, he could cheer you up. But now he can be part of the celebration since everything turned out in our favor. I had my dad search for a puppy while we were away, and he brought him over here. You always wanted a dog," Pearl said.

"I'm going to name him, Jeff," Joe said. "After someone I knew in the war who was a good guy but a little wild." Joe thought back to the young soldier who was always willing to volunteer.

"I know how much you love to hunt," Pearl said. "I thought you could train him to go along with you. He should be a good dog for bird hunting."

"Thank you, Pearl. You knocked me off my feet with this little guy. He's perfect," Joe said gratefully. Jeff cocked his head to one side and looked up at his new master.

On Monday, March 6th, after the trade with Cleveland was completed, Joe reported for duty in Boston. Joe and Pearl found an apartment in Cambridge. They couldn't afford to live on the Back Bay closest to the stadium. Joe enjoyed walking across the bridge to get to the stadium anyway. He had a bridge to cross on his way to work in most of the cities he had lived in leading up to this one. Ball parks always seemed to be near rivers.

When Joe arrived at Fenway for the first time and walked down the dark tunnel out onto the field, he stood at first base all by himself and took it all in. He smelled the cut grass and the freshly raked dirt along the baselines. He saw the new seats that had just been installed in the grandstands. Joe looked in awe at the huge wooden wall behind left field covered in advertisements. Leading up to the wall was a 10-foot-high mound of dirt. The right field fence was much closer than the left. The American flag was flying from the flagpole behind center field under a bright blue sky. Fenway had such an intimate feel to it, and Joe thought he could hit a lot of home runs in this park.

Joe put on his uniform in the clubhouse and couldn't help but hold up the red socks that went with the uniform. He recalled the first pair of colored socks he had put on all those years ago in McKeesport. He had come a long way from that first game he played. Joe met up with a few reporters from the Boston Globe and told them, "I'm very glad to be with the Red Sox. And I plan to give Duffy the best I have."

Manager Hugh Duffy was a no-nonsense coach. He made the Red Sox players take care of their own uniforms on the road. It went back to his days when he was a pitcher in the league. Duffy also decided to use Joe in left field rather than at first base. Joe made some great catches in left field, a few of them on that mound of dirt under the scoreboard, and the crowds cheered. He had to get his war-weary legs used to running up and down that mound to field balls.

In one of their first games on the road, Joe opened with a left field homer. They were playing against the Minneapolis Millers in Tennessee. Joe had a few fans in the crowd from his Chattanooga Lookout days. He didn't disappoint them when he tripled on his next time at bat. He covered every inch of left field, and the Sox won the game 5 to 2.

Because Joe was on the road so much, he tried to take Pearl out when they were at home. They walked from their apartment in Cambridge down Massachusetts Avenue to the new Loew's

State Theatre. It had just opened in March, and neither Joe nor Pearl could believe how beautiful it was. When they were seated in the exquisite, red velvet seats, Pearl kept looking all around her at the ornate gold walls and ceilings.

"My billiard parlour is nothing compared to this," Joe whispered to Pearl as the lights lowered and the organ played.

They were seeing Blood and Sand starring the dashing Rudolf Valentino. Valentino played Juan Gallardo, a poor boy who grew up to become one of the greatest matadors in Spain. Joe saw parallels to his own life in the film.

Pearl flinched at the bullfighting scenes. Joe put his arm around her, and she hid her face in his shoulder. He didn't enjoy seeing the bulls treated that way either. Both Joe and Pearl loved animals.

Joe played ball through the summer, and the crowds at Fenway Park continued to cheer for him. He was in the newspaper almost every day. Sometimes there were cartoons making fun of his weak legs, his crouching stance, or his scarred face, but Joe kept his sense of humor and laughed at himself.

1924

J oe could hardly wait to show Pearl the piece about him in
the *Pittsburgh Press*. The reporter mailed a copy to him
after their talk. He was sure his father and brothers had
seen this because they got the paper in Coulters. He was also
happy that his old friend from Cleveland, Lee Fohl, had replaced Hugh Duffy as the manager for the Red Sox.

Pittsburgh Press, 20 January 1924

JOE HARRIS PREDICTS GREAT YEAR FOR BOL-
STERED BOSTON AMERICANS AND PLANS RALLY
OF HIS OWN TOO

With a substantial increase in salary and assurance that
as possible captain of the team he will have the loyal back-
ing of the Boston fans and the ardent support of the Red Sox
management, Joe Harris is "all set" for what he declares is
going to be the best year he has ever had in organized baseball.

"If I don't come through this year, I'll be disappointed,
for the situation was never brighter than it is right now," he
declared.

Though not yet officially designated captain, there is every prospect that he will be. Ever since the Cleveland-Boston trade was announced and it was stated that Harris was to play first base, the papers in the Bean City have been mentioning Joe repeatedly for the place of captain. There is every assurance, it seems, that he will land the post, too.

"We are going to have a bang-up team this year," he told his interviewer. "It couldn't be otherwise. The Red Sox have the edge in this deal, and to my way of thinking the players we have obtained have batting and fielding records that can't help but put the Sox on the map."

Harris says Boston fans treated him royally the moment he had come to terms with Robert Quinn, president of the team, and had signed his contract. Talking about a possible lineup, he submitted a list that included Steve O'Neill, catcher; Bill Wambsganss, second; Dudley Lee, of Tulsa, shortstop; Bobby Veach, left field; MacMillan, third; Harris, first; Flagstead, right; and Boone, middle field. The Boone who is shifted to the outfield, Harris says, is a brother of the Boone who pitches. The outfielder was obtained from San Antonio in exchange for Reichle. Referring to pitchers, he ventured the assertion:

"You are going to look a long time before you find more promising material than Murray and Piercy."

The pitchers and catchers are due to leave for San Antonio training camp, where the Red Sox will train this year, on February 20, he said, and O'Neill, Jack Quinn, Bobby Veach, Wamby, and Harris will go to Hot Springs on February 10. "We'll be in San Antonio with the regulars on March 1, that's sure," said Harris; "anyhow, those are our instructions."

Joe kept smiling his satisfaction all through the interview. It is no secret that he would have liked to go to Cleveland, but conditions have so switched around, with his old friend, Lee Fohl, in charge of affairs, that he is perfectly content to stay with the Sox.

"We are going to have an aggregation this year that will do some batting," he declared. Asked if he would be in the cleanup position, he said, "Not necessarily. We have four or five good stickers for that place. The fact is, we won't have to worry so much about our batting this year. Nearly everyone on the team is a good sticker," and he called attention to the batting averages of Bobby Veach, Wamby, and O'Neill, to illustrate. It is a coincidence that Harris and O'Neill, who is also a pal of his, are of the same age, 32. Wamby is 29, and Veach, who has been in the game a good many years, is 35.

Harris is delighted that O'Neill is going to be with the team. "Ten years is too long for a ball player in any town," Harris ventured, "and I believe O'Neill was ready and anxious to go when the chance came, though I know there never was a more loyal player to the Cleveland team than he. He will certainly be an asset to the Red Sox, and so I feel sure with such material as we have—and good sticking, at that—we have a right to be optimistic over the Red Sox chances. Certainly, we will do our best to stay out of the cellar."

\#

"I guess I'm married to a real celebrity now," Pearl said as she finished reading the article.

"Didn't you know that when you came calling to the billiard parlour in Franklin?"

Joe teased her. She swatted Joe playfully with the rolled-up newspaper.

Joe and Pearl realized their celebrity when they were invited to stay at the mansion of a prominent meat packer in Boston, Carl Rodman, when Joe returned from spring training and the season started. They moved out of their Cambridge apartment. Pearl spent time shopping and playing cards with Carl's wife, Sophia. The meat packer took Joe to play 30 holes of golf and introduced Joe to all his friends as "Captain Joe Harris."

It felt cold enough to snow as the Red Sox took the field at Fenway to play their opening day game against the New York Yankees. Before the game, a band, a platoon of Marines, and the two teams marched to the flagpole. The players held their hats over their hearts as the American flag was unfurled to the sounds of the band playing the National Anthem. Beneath the American flag was a white pennant bearing the Red Sox logo. The stands were cheerfully decorated with red, white, and blue bunting and streamers. Joe could smell the mulch in the new landscape gardening around the pitchers' box and behind home plate.

The thousands who sat in the stands saw a brilliantly pitched game with the Sox scoring only one run in the fifth inning. Joe walked in the fifth inning, so he had no hits to contribute to the team. Despite that, it looked like the perfect opening afternoon.

Big "Babe" Ruth, who many in the stands had come to see, received a roaring ovation when he first stepped up to bat even though he struck out. Then he was walked and on the third trip hit a lofty foul for Steve O'Neill, the new catcher for the Sox and Joe's old friend. Joe was delighted that his team was putting Babe in his place. But Babe was the first hitter for the Yankees in the ninth, and he made that at bat count when he hit a line drive to right field to start all the Red Sox trouble. Babe hurt his legs going down to second and rolled with pain. The crowd cheered when he stood up and brushed himself off. The Yankee first baseman, Wally Pipp, followed Ruth's hit with a sacrifice. Wamby, the Sox second baseman, lost a little hopper sent his way by Bob Meusel, the Yankee right fielder, and Meusel was on base. Wally Schang, the Yankee catcher, was up next. He hit towards Wamby and there was a chance for a double play. But Wamby again missed the ball, couldn't even pick it up. Meusel rushed around third base and came in standing up. The Yankees won the game.

The opening game was an exception to Joe's usual hitting prowess. After Joe's bat was described as "poison" to the other teams in a couple of news articles, Joe got an interesting letter in the mail from the Hillerich & Bradsby Co., sole manufacturers of the celebrated "Louisville Slugger" baseball bats. They offered Joe a contract to make signature Louisville Slugger bats for him for the next twenty years. All of the players coveted the white ash and hard maple bats. Every child at Fenway Park who was a fan of Joe's could use the exact same bat that he used in the games.

The contract read:

In consideration of One Dollar ($1.00) and other good and valuable considerations in hand paid, and receipt of which is hereby acknowledged, I, the undersigned, hereby give and grant unto Hillerich & Bradsby Co., a corporation of Kentucky, its successors and assigns, the sole and exclusive right for Twenty (20) years from date, the use of my name, autograph, portrait, photograph, picture, initials and/or nickname, for trademark and/or advertising purposes in connection with the manufacture and/or sale of baseball bats, and I hereby consent to the registration thereof as a trademark for baseball bats by said Hillerich & Bradsby Co.

I hereby warrant that I have not previously given my consent to any agreement in any ways in conflict with this foregoing.

Executed in duplicate this 14th day of June, 1924.

Joe signed the contract and they used the image of his signature on the bat's handle. He liked the medium sized barrel on the custom bat that H & B made for him. Joe placed several inches of tape about 8 to 10 inches up the handle to improve his grip. The bat had a large hitting surface that helped Joe with his batting average of .350. Joe had a batch of the bats with his signature on them that he kept for years.

Joe also got a letter from the American Tobacco Company with a $10 check in it for the rights to use his image on a baseball card. The baseball cards were used as stiffeners in cigarette packages. Joe didn't like that kids had to get the cards from cigarette packs but he reluctantly went along with it.

It wasn't all good fortune though. Right at this same time in June, Steve and Joe were dressing in the locker room after a game against Columbus. "My throat is really hurting and I think I have a fever," Joe said to Steve.

"Sure, and you should be talking to the doctor. Hey Doc," Steve said.

"What is it?" Dr. Joy, the team doctor, asked. Dr. Joy's stethoscope dangled from his neck. He had deep, dark brown eyes peering out from black framed glasses. His sandy brown hair was parted on one side with wisps trying to fly away here and there.

"Joe, here, fancies himself with a sore throat," Steve said.

"Let me have a look," Dr. Joy said. He bent Joe's head back and looked into his throat with a small flashlight that he carried in his pocket.

"Mmm. Those tonsils are infected and will have to come out," Dr. Joy said. "We'll do it here in Columbus, and then you can head home to Franklin for a while to recuperate."

While Joe was recovering from the procedure, he got painful neuritis in his back and left arm. Joe thought it was connected to the tonsils, but Dr. Joy assured him it was inflammation of the nerves as a result of his war injuries. Joe wanted to get his full strength back before returning to the field. The doctor kept him in the hospital and applied warm plasters to his back to stimulate his muscles and promote healing. Joe had to write letters to Pearl to keep her up to date as she stayed in Boston with the Rodmans while he was in the hospital.

At the end of June, Joe returned to Boston. Joe told Pearl, "I'm feeling fine, except that now my legs have been rather weak. I think the plaster on my back helped to iron out the kinks, but my legs still aren't as strong as they used to be. You know I want to get back to practicing with the team."

"If I know your 'never say die' attitude," Pearl said, "You'll be back as the Slugger of the team in no time."

Joe and Pearl walked slowly in Boston Common every day. They would enter through the Charles Street Gate and walk the newly paved walkways to the Frog Pond. They sat and held hands on one of the benches as they gazed at the fountain cascading umbrella-like in the middle of the pond. Pearl appreciated the walks because she wanted to help Joe gradually increase his strength, but she also enjoyed the onlookers watching her walk with her celebrity husband.

Joe noticed a young boy and his mother who came to the park every day at the same time. After a few days, they approached Joe and Pearl as they were sitting on the bench. The boy was wearing a white baseball cap with a red bill and kept his head down.

"Aren't you Joe Harris, the Moon?" the boy asked shyly, peeking out from under the bill of his cap.

"Yes, I am," said Joe.

"I told my mommy that was you," the little boy said. "I brought along my baseball card today. Would you sign it?"

"Sure, I'll sign it," Joe said as he took the card from the boy. The card showed him holding the mitt in front of his face. Joe signed it across the bottom, Moon Harris.

"Thanks, Moon!" the child exclaimed joyfully as he ran off to join his mother again. Joe and Pearl looked at each other and smiled.

Despite how hard Joe was trying when he returned to the game, the Red Sox finished the season near the bottom of the league in seventh place out of eight teams. He had hoped to keep them out of the cellar but was not successful. Cleveland finished ahead of Boston. As much as Joe loved his new hometown of Boston, Joe wished he could have stayed and played for Cleveland when he was reinstated. Now the number one team in the league was the Washington Senators. Joe dreamed of playing for a number one team.

Chapter Fifteen

1925

O n April 22nd Joe was feeling much healthier and ready to play in the opening home game for the Red Sox against the Philadelphia Athletics. He had taken baths in the hot springs while he was in training. He rested at the beginning of the year, and he was excited about being in front of the fans again.

The field at Fenway Park looked picture perfect, and the weather as good as expected for the opener in April in Boston. Coughlin's 101st Regimental Band and two Army officers took part in the flag raising. Massachusetts Governor Fuller threw out the first pitch.

The game was tied and in the tenth inning, Joe got up to bat facing their southpaw pitcher. Joe hoped to get them out of this desperate situation, but with the scarring on his eye from the war, it was difficult to see the pitches. Joe struck out. The crowd's rooting was in vain as the Sox ended up losing the game 5 to 6.

Joe came off the field at the end of the game to talk to his manager and friend, Lee Fohl. "Look, Joe," Lee said. "I think you're having some trouble with your eye and I'm going to play Todt at first base for a while."

"But I'm changing my stance. Doing more of a crouch," Joe said. "It helps. It really does." Joe was the type of batter who crowded the plate and choked the bat slightly. He was an excellent judge of good pitches. He picked out pitches that looked good, made a quick slash, and caused the opposing team real trouble if it connected. But like all good hitters who take a healthy swing, Joe sometimes retired on strikes.

"I'm sorry, buddy," Lee said. "I know you're trying."

"Just keep me in the game, Lee," Joe asked.

"There's also the problem with your base running. You're going slower and slower," Lee said. "I have to keep you on the bench for a while."

Shortly after the opener and after being benched for a while, Joe's reputation put him back in the game. On April 30th Joe found out the Red Sox traded him to the Washington Senators, the first-place team in the league. Joe had heard rumors of the trade before it went through. Joe was heading to Griffith Field in Washington, DC.

Griffith Field was laid out at an angle compared to the surrounding streets. A large double-decked concrete pier had replaced the left field bleachers. A high wall was across the right field, but it was not as imposing as the wall at Fenway. Joe looked up to see the National Bohemian beer sign, in the shape of a beer bottle, 56 feet above the playing field. Because they were in Washington, DC, there was a presidential box near the first base dugout. Every president since William H. Taft had thrown out a ceremonial first pitch at least once. If Joe was lucky, he may get to shake the hand of President Calvin Coolidge. Or even better, get to meet the First Lady, Grace

Coolidge. She was a great Boston Red Sox fan and would probably remember Joe from his games in Boston.

Joe liked the Senators' uniforms, too. They were white with red pinstripes on both the shirt and pants with a red "W" on the sleeve. The knicker pants were loose fitting and comfortable.

The owner of the Senators, Clark Griffith, introduced Joe to his new manager. "Joe Harris, I'd like you to meet Bucky Harris," Griffith said. Joe shook Bucky's hand.

"Are you two related?" Griffith asked.

"I don't think so," Joe replied to Griffith. "Where are you from?" Joe asked Bucky.

"I was born in New Jersey," Bucky said. "My father emigrated from Wales. But we moved to Pittston, Pennsylvania, near Scranton, when I was 6 years old."

"You look like you're only a little over 6 years old now," Joe joked. Bucky was only 29 years old and the youngest manager in the league. He was the same height as Joe, but only weighed about 150 pounds and had a baby face.

"I had to quit school to work in the coal mines," Bucky said.

"Well, I'll be damned," Joe said. "What a coincidence. I had to do that, too. I worked in the mines in Coulters, Pennsylvania. But that's on the other side of the state from Scranton."

"But I loved playing baseball. And that got me out of the mines when a scout saw me play," Bucky said.

"It's like you're telling my story," Joe said to him. "Maybe our families were related back in the UK. My father is from a little village called Blore Hall. In Staffordshire, England."

"Tell Joe how you got the nickname, Bucky," Griffith said.

"Not only do I love baseball, I also love basketball. I play basketball at the YMCA to keep in shape and build up my strength. Anyway, in one rough game I had a coupla' players riding on my back. When I shook 'em off and made a shot, one of my friends said I bucked like a bronco. My friends started calling me 'Bucky' and the name stuck. To tell you the truth, I like it better than Stanley." Bucky laughed.

Joe played regularly in the outfield for the whole month of May, but during that time he was only hitting .280. He expected much more of himself because he slammed the ball when he played for the Red Sox. In one game against Philadelphia he performed brilliantly at bat, but overall his playing was a dis-appointment. It was difficult for him to keep up the pace. In a June twelve inning game against the Yankees, Bucky had to pull Joe after the eighth inning. This really irked Joe because he was playing against Babe Ruth, and he knew in his heart that he could outhit him.

In July, Joe begged Bucky to put him back in the game when they were playing against his old team, the Red Sox.

"Bucky, I know Fenway Park. I can hit it out of there," Joe begged.

"Okay, I will give you a chance. But only because I think you will intimidate some of your old teammates," Bucky said.

In the first inning, with two men on base, Joe knocked the ball over the left field fence and chased right fielder, Sam Rice, and left fielder, Goose Goslin, over the plate. In the fifth inning, Joe doubled and was brought in with a clever bunt by the catcher, Muddy Ruel. Joe made three double plays in the out-field. In the end, the Senators were victorious over Joe's old Red Sox team 11 to 0.

In August, Joe got a phone call from Pearl. Now that Joe was playing with Washington, Pearl had to move out of the Rodman's mansion and back to their winter home in Franklin while Joe was in different towns playing ball. His pointer, Jeff, had run off somewhere, and she couldn't find him. Pearl didn't want Joe to worry, but because they had no children, Jeff had become like a child to them. So, she knew she had to tell him that Jeff had run off.

"Pearl, put an ad in the newspaper and offer a reward," Joe said.

"Okay, honey, I'll do that." Pearl said. "I'm happy you're doing so well in Washington, now. I know you had a little rough spot, but it seems like you're back to your old self. I read about you in the Franklin paper all the time."

"Pearl, I'm sure this team is heading to the World Series. This is what I've been preparing for my whole life. I can't let myself get distracted now by old Jeff," Joe said.

"Please, just concentrate on your baseball. Don't worry about Jeff. I'll find him," Pearl said, trying to sound more confident than she was. Pearl thought to herself, *It's just as well I never had a child. I can't even keep track of a dog.*

"I hope you do, Pearl. Why did this have to happen now? That dog means the world to me," Joe said.

"I'll find him. I promise I will," Pearl said.

"When you find him, and the baseball season is over, I'm going to take him on the longest hunt ever. He'll never want to run away again," Joe said.

Joe had only been playing for the Senators for 6 months when they went to the World Series. Bucky and the rest of the team were surprised when October 7th was declared "Joe Harris Day" at Forbes Field on the first day of the World Series between the Pirates and the Senators. Joe was quite a celebrity in the Pittsburgh area, but he was playing for the Senators, so the team didn't quite understand why they were celebrating him in Pittsburgh.

When Joe arrived at Forbes Field early in the day, he saw that lines of fans were forming. Along with his heart pounding in his chest, all the skin on his body was tingling. He pulled his jacket collar up around his neck to ward off the chilly breeze, but the sky looked clear for the game. He and Pearl had driven to the game with his friend Jim Borland, the sportswriter from Franklin. It had been sixteen years since the Pirates were in the World Series.

"Joe, Franklin natives are paying $50 to see you, their hometown hero, play in the World Series game," Jim said to him. "They chartered a bus to come."

"I'm honored, Jim," Joe said humbly. "I'll do my best not to let them down."

"The Washington players' wives are insisting we all sit together," Pearl said. "I'd much rather sit in the crowd with the Franklin townies."

"I'll hear you cheering wherever you're sitting," Joe said, as he put his hand on the small of Pearl's back to usher her through the crowd.

When some fans in the line saw Joe arrive, they immediately started chanting, "Moon, Moon, Moon!" Joe walked down the line at the entrance, nodded his head, shook hands, and signed the occasional baseball along the way. His fans called after him.

"Good luck, Moon."

"You're a champion, Moon."

"Would you sign my baseball, Moon?"

"Give it all you've got, Moon."

"Hit hard. Run fast. Remember to turn left, Moon."

Joe could not control his smile.

Washington beat Pittsburgh 4 to 1 in that game. At Joe's first at bat in the second inning, he hit the only home run to put

Washington on the scoreboard. He was happy to do that in front of so many of his fans, and his fans seemed to enjoy watching him do so well even though he was on the opposing team.

In Game 3, the Series moved back to Griffith Stadium in Washington. It was Joe's single in this game that brought in the winning run. But it was in Game 4 where Joe shined again. No matter what came to him—fast balls, hooks, knuckle balls—Joe sent them all back over the fences. Joe hit two home runs, and Walter Johnson, the pitcher for the Senators, pitched a no-hitter. Left fielder Goose Goslin hit the other two home runs to give the Senators the 4 to 0 win.

At that point, the Senators took a 3 to 1 Series lead. Pittsburgh won Game 5 with a score of 6 to 3 in Washington. Joe hit a home run in the fourth inning to tie the game, but the Pirates came back to win and force a Game 6. They won again in Game 6 with a score of 3 to 2 in Pittsburgh. The Pirates second baseman Eddie Moore was the hero of that game when he bounced a home run to the left field bleachers.

The series was postponed twice for bad weather as the teams readied themselves to play Game 7. Not only was there a steady downpour at Forbes Field, there was also the yellow glow from the steel mills along the Monongahela River. They played Game 7 in probably the worst conditions ever for a World Series game. The infield was a sea of mud. Several times pitcher Walter Johnson had to carry sawdust in his cap as he walked, bare-headed, to the mound with rain pouring down on him.

Goose Goslin and Joe were standing next to each other in the dugout. Joe asked, "Can you believe how much fog there is? I've lived here most of my life and never seen anything like this."

"I couldn't even see the infield during the last three innings," Goose answered.

Twice in Game 7 the visiting Senators had leads over the Pirates but failed to hold them. The Pirates hit Walter Johnson, the "Big Train," for 15 hits. The Big Train's fast ball worked great until it got wet, and then he lost control of it. He bowed his grey head to his chest at the end of the game.

Automobiles blaring car horns and loud singing went on into the night in Pittsburgh as the World Series win thrilled the fans. Fifth Avenue was completely blocked by pedestrians all night long. Bucky Harris was buried in effigy, after his corpse was carried through town by half a dozen pallbearers as the crowd roared. Although Joe was playing for the losing team, he couldn't help but feel a little pride for his hometown.

After Joe's hitting .440 in the Series, the Senators offered him a three-year contract with the American League at $8,000 per year.

In November, with the Series behind him, Joe made good on his promise to go hunting in western Pennsylvania and then to have a game dinner with the spoils of his hunt. Joe was relieved that Pearl had been successful in finding his pointer, Jeff. A local man returned the dog after Pearl offered a $500 reward for him. Joe enjoyed showing Jeff's pointing skills to his friends. The dog would stand like a statue in the field. Joe invited Bill McKechnie, manager of the Pirates, Jack Onslow, a Pirates coach, and Jim Borland, his sportswriter friend, to go along with him on his three-day long rabbit and deer hunt. A few inches of snow had fallen, which made the hunting great.

When Joe and the others returned from the woods to the Park Hotel where he and Pearl had an apartment, Pearl made a great hunt dinner for the men. On Pearl's wrist a diamond bracelet glittered as she served up the roasted rabbit, potatoes, and carrots.

Bill McKechnie commented, "Where did you get that fancy diamond bracelet, Pearl?"

"You know, even though Joe was on the losing side of the series, his Franklin fans love him. They made him a special diamond World Series ring, very similar to yours. So, he bought me a matching bracelet," Pearl smiled.

Joe held out his hand to show off his ring. The center of the ring had the words "1925 World Series" engraved in a circle. Around the circle was a baseball diamond with a diamond at each base. A crossed pair of baseball bats was at the base.

"Maybe next year we can get you on the winning side," Bill joked.

"There's something else we have to talk about tonight," Jim Borland said as he passed the bowl of potatoes around the table.

"What's that?" Joe asked. He poured each of his guests another glass of red wine.

"I received this letter at the offices of the paper from a young boy, Jasper Reed, from Beaver Falls. He's in the hospital and very sick. But he's a great fan of yours. Listens to all the games on the radio. From the looks of his writing, he's probably 11 or 12 years old," Jim said.

"He'd like to have an autographed baseball from you for Christmas," Jim continued.

Joe got up from the table and went to the curio cabinet in the front room. He took out a baseball autographed by every player on the Washington team. He brought it back to the table.

"Oh, Joe, that's one of your prized possessions," Pearl exclaimed.

"That ought to make any boy happy," Joe said as he tossed the ball across the table to Jim. Joe enjoyed playing Santa Claus.

Chapter Sixteen

1926

With his bonus money from the World Series, Joe had plastic surgery in January to repair his eye. At the end of the month, he returned to his apartment in the Park Hotel in Franklin to recuperate from the surgery. Surgeons grafted skin from the nape of Joe's neck to his face. They transferred a slight piece of his eyelid to a spot below his eye. The vivid scar, which marred the side of his face and stretched down diagonally from the corner of his eye, disappeared. When the doctor removed the bandages after a week, Joe's face was almost as it had been before that fateful day in Argonne, France. After the operation, Joe smiled again. Before the operation Joe had to sight the balls thrown to him from his right eye only. Now, with the scar gone, he had unobstructed vision out of both eyes again.

Joe sat quietly in the apartment and looked out of the window. Pearl had never seen him so quiet and pensive before. "What is bothering you, honey?" she asked.

"I know that my face has looked like the side of a craggy mountain," he said. "But that's the face you fell in love with. What if you don't like the way I look anymore?"

"Oh, Joe, I didn't fall in love with you for your looks. I fell in love with you for your adventurous spirit and how you always live in the moment. I'll be with you through anything life has to offer. I'm just happy that you will be able to see me better." Pearl said.

Joe grabbed hold of Pearl's hand and pulled her into his lap. She laughed and then kissed him gently where the scar had been. His pointer, Jeff, barked and tried to jump up on both of them. Joe scratched Jeff behind his floppy ears and then hugged his wife.

In April, before he left for the Senators' training camp in Tampa, Joe got a call from Lawrence Gent, his partner in the Grand Hotel.

"Joe, I have some good news and some bad news." Mr. Gent said. "What do you want to hear first?"

"Tell me the bad news," Joe said.

"Well, I'm having some health issues, and I have to retire from running the Grand Hotel," Mr. Gent said.

"You work hard. You deserve to retire, so I don't think that's such bad news," Joe said. "What's the good news?"

"I've found a buyer for the hotel. And, of course, they will buy the billiard parlour and bowling alley, too. You will become a very wealthy man after this sale," Mr. Gent said.

"You've always been fair to me and given me sound business advice," Joe said. "So just tell me where and when to sign the papers." Joe would now have a little nest egg, but he would also have to rely on the money he made as a baseball player only for his living expenses. He and his baseball buddies could still hang out at the parlour, but he wouldn't have that income as a safety net anymore.

Now the newspapers in Franklin were reporting more on Babe Ruth and his comeback rather than on Joe's accomplishments. Babe Ruth packed them in at every Yankees game. Even when he played in exhibition games, it was standing room only. Ruth became the greatest slugger in baseball in 1921 when he broke the record with 59 home runs. He had a slump and tried his hand at acting in vaudeville for a few years. But this year he was back with the Yankees after much conditioning in the gym playing handball. He was down to 212 pounds according to all the papers.

In July Babe Ruth attempted to catch a "skyball" thrown from an airplane flying at 700 feet above Mitchell Field in Long Island. He was attempting to outdo Gabby Street's catch of a ball thrown from the Washington Monument. Joe could only shake his head at the thought of such a gimmick.

It was in July, too, that Joe found out his manager Bucky Harris and Senators owner Clark Griffith put him on waivers. After finding out that many clubs were interested in him, though, the Senators kept him so that he wouldn't go to a rival team, at least until the close of the season.

Joe's brief comeback after his eye operation brought to mind his heyday with the Two Team league in Franklin when the fans loved to watch him. Not as flamboyant as the Babe's comeback, but many newspapers showed photographs of his newly repaired face. The owner of the Franklin Motor Sales Company surprised Joe when he asked him to pose next to the Essex "6" Coach automobile for a newspaper advertisement in his hometown. The Essex boasted fine performance, smooth and more powerful operation, and striking precision just like Joe the Moon Harris who stood dressed in a dashing suit on its sideboard. The owner gave the $819 vehicle to Joe in exchange for his endorsement. It delighted Pearl. Despite these small successes, Joe still constantly compared himself to Ruth. The trials of his fame seemed to keep his life in constant upheaval.

When October rolled around, Joe's old team, the Boston Red Sox, was at the bottom of the American League. The Washington Senators were in the middle of the pack at fourth place. And Babe Ruth's Yankees were at the top. The Yankees played the St. Louis Cardinals in the 1926 World Series. There would be no World Series game for Joe this year.

Joe and Pearl were reading the paper at breakfast when Pearl called Joe's attention to a picture in the paper of an adolescent boy with a swollen eye. "Look at this, Joe. This little boy, Johnny Sylvester, got kicked in the head by a horse and then got an infection. He's very sick. His father was supposed to take him to a World Series game, but now he can't go. Babe Ruth sent him an autographed baseball that says, 'I'll knock a homer for you,' in addition to his autograph. It reminds me of that little boy last year, Jasper Reed, who wanted a baseball from you."

"If I was playing in this World Series this year, I'd knock a homer for Jasper. And Johnny, too," Joe said wistfully, looking at the picture of young Johnny in the paper.

"I know you would," Pearl said as she poured him another cup of coffee and kissed the top of his head.

Joe listened to the Series on the radio. In Game 4, played in St. Louis, Babe Ruth hit three home runs. In the sixth inning, with two home runs already in the game, Babe Ruth came up to the plate. The announcers on the radio at the game said:

"The Babe is up. Two home runs today. One ball, far outside. Babe's shoulders look as if there is murder in them down there, the way he is swinging that bat down there. A high foul into the left field stands. That great big bat of

Babe's looks like a toothpick down there, he is so big himself. Here it is. Babe shot a bad one and fouled it. Two strikes and one ball. The outfield have all moved very far towards right. It is coming up now. A little too close. Two strikes and two balls. He has got two home runs and a base on balls so far today. Here it is, and a ball. Three and two. The Babe is waving that wand of his over the plate. Bell is loosening up his arm. The Babe is hit clear into the center field bleachers for a home run! For a home run! Did you hear what I said? Where is that fellow who told me not to talk about Ruth anymore? Send him up here.

Oh, what a shot! Directly over second. The boys are all over him over there. One of the boys is riding on Ruth's back. Oh, what a shot! Directly over second base, far into the bleachers out in center field, and almost on a line, and then that dumbbell, where is he, who told me not to talk about Ruth. Oh, boy! Not that I love Ruth, but oh, how I love to see a shot like that! Wow! That is a World Series record. Three home runs in one World Series game and what a home run! That was probably the longest hit ever in Sportsman's Park. They tell me this is the first ball ever hit in the center field stand. That is a mile and half from here. You know what I mean."

Joe read in the newspaper the next day that the ball Babe Ruth hit had crashed through the window of an auto dealer across the street from the stadium. Joe had to admit that sometimes Ruth's every day playing was more fantastic than those made-up tricks he did for publicity's sake. And he made good on his promise and hit a homer for Johnny Sylvester.

The Yankees and the Cardinals played the deciding Game 7 on October 10th in Yankee Stadium. The Yankees scored the first run of the game in the third inning with a Babe Ruth home run. In the following inning, the Cardinals came back to take a 3 to 1 lead. In the sixth inning, the Yankees cut the Cardinals lead by scoring Jumping Joe Dugan. In the bottom of the ninth, with two outs and needing to preserve the Cardinals slim lead, Cardinals pitcher Grover Cleveland Alexander faced Ruth. Ruth had hit that solo home run but also walked three times. The announcer said:

"The count went to three and two. Ruth was swaying eagerly. The soupbone creaked again. The ball seemed a fraction of an inch from being a strike. Ruth paused for a moment. Even he was uncertain. Then he trotted down to first."

With two outs and Ruth walked to first base, left fielder Bob Meusel came up to the plate, with Lou Gehrig on deck behind him. Just as Meusel was about to take his first pitch, Ruth made the bold move of trying to steal second base. The entire crowd gasped at once, and Joe moved to the edge of his chair as he listened at home. Meusel swung and missed. Cardinals catcher Bob O'Farrell immediately threw to second base. Again, the announcer:

"Ruth is walked for the fourth time today. One strike on Bob Meusel. Going down to second! The game is over! Babe tried to steal second and is put out catcher to second!"

Ruth's failed attempt to steal second ended the series, and the Cardinals had won. Joe settled back in his chair and smirked smugly at the radio. Joe's dog curled on the floor beside him, looked up at him for a moment, and yawned.

Chapter Seventeen

1927

Joe started the year by signing his contract with the Washington Senators. Though he was out in the woods hunting nearly every day over the winter, tramping up and down the western Pennsylvania hills, Joe had gained about 25 pounds. Joe knew that weight would have to come off during spring training. He was far from great physical shape.

Yet another disappointment faced Joe when he got news that his father died on January 12th. Joe always felt being named after his father was a badge of honor, even though his father had never been to one of his games. At the beginning of Joe's career, his father couldn't afford to attend his games in far off cities. And later when Joe could pay his father's way, he didn't like traveling to different cities like his gallivanting son. For Joe's dad, his home was comfort to him, where he knew all the routines.

In February, Joe achieved his childhood dream of playing with the Pittsburgh Pirates when his contract was purchased by Pittsburgh for $10,000. It was the most money Joe had ever made. After three unsuccessful attempts to acquire Joe, Pittsburgh owner Barney Dreyfuss renewed his negotiations when he learned that the Washington Senators had signed Tris Speaker and probably didn't need Joe as a utility player anymore. Dreyfus didn't want to see Joe get sent back down to the minor leagues. It thrilled Joe and Pearl to be in Pittsburgh, so close to their Franklin home. Now that he could get home more frequently during the playing season, Joe didn't mind getting on the train to leave snowy Franklin for training camp in sunny Paso Robles, California.

"I'm tickled to death to be with the Pirates. I'm well satisfied with the whole deal, and you can tell the fans for me that I'm going to try my best to satisfy them, because I'm home now," Joe said to the banquet guests at the Chatham Hotel in Pittsburgh where he was the guest of honor. The banquet was to honor Company I, 320th Infantry, 80th Division, but it also coincided with the news of Joe's trade between the American League Washington Senators and the National League Pittsburgh Pirates.

"My parents are gone now," Joe continued, "but I have a lot of relatives in and around Pittsburgh. I'm going to play for my hometown just as hard as I can. I'm just tickled kinny to be here!"

To his former service members at the banquet, Joe was not just Joe Harris, but Joe the Moon Harris. The Moon had stepped into his lieutenant's shoes when they were trapped in a trench and he became the fighter they all saw on the baseball field.

Sergeant Charles E. Potts stood up at the banquet to talk about the Moon. "There were a lot of baseball players with the American army in France, but there never was a baseball player who saw the service and the fighting that Harris did with us. We were shock troops in Pershing's First Army."

"It was a way back," Potts continued, "yet it doesn't seem so long ago. In September of 1918, only a couple of months before the Armistice was signed, we were going hard at it up front. Sergeant Joe Harris, behind a trench mortar, was second in command to Lieutenant Zouck. Zouck was a wonderful man and well liked, but he was killed that morning. And everything was left up to Harris with his four squads of eight men each. He got in there and fought as he never fought before—and with the enemy less than 100 yards away. The boys will always remember him for his fine spirit in that engagement."

"There wasn't a better or braver soldier in the whole army than Harris. He proved he was a real fighter and a real buddy. And after you've lived with a man for two years, that's just the way we look at it, we were just a big family, you know him. And don't think for a minute that there's a single fellow here tonight that doesn't realize that Harris is just as much of a soldier as he is a baseball player."

There were tears in the eyes of a lot of the men as they congratulated the guest of honor. Joe had a lump in his throat as he thought about all the men he left behind.

Joe knew he was the oldest man on the Pirates team. But in the '25 World Series, when he played with the Senators against the Pirates, he batted .440 against the Pirate pitchers. He made 11 hits in 25 times at bat, including a couple of home runs. He felt like he could still hold his own on the team.

In July Joe found out that his war buddy Johnny Miljus was coming to pitch for the Pirates from the Seattle Indians.

"I can't believe we're going to be back together again, Johnny," Joe felt so joyful that he thought his heart would explode. Joe put his hand on the back of Johnny's neck and shook him a few times. It had been almost ten years since they had been together in France, but he felt Johnny was like a brother to him.

"It's great to be back together again," Johnny said, but he had a troubled look on his face.

"What's wrong, my friend?"

"Joe, the Seattle club wouldn't even pay for my wife's transportation back East," Johnny said.

"Mr. Dreyfuss will pay for it, Johnny," Joe told him. "He's the most generous team owner I ever worked for. He's a good man. He didn't want to see me get put back down in the minors and he bought my contract from Washington."

Joe was having some stomach trouble and dizzy spells in July. Joe's absence on the field threw the Pirates' infield out of kilter. Joe thought he had eaten some clams in New York that may have been the culprit. Dreyfus gave Joe some slack because Joe's hitting throughout the year made the Pirates contenders in the National League pennant race. The Waner brothers, Paul and Lloyd, and Joe had saved the Pirates.

Many Pittsburgh fans knew that Joe was key to winning them the pennant. Most of the fans satisfied themselves with reading the box scores and following their favorite player's statistics in the newspapers. One of Joe's fans, James Watson, wrote an acrostic poem about his hero, titled 'J-O-E H-A-R-R-I-S,' and it was printed in the *Pittsburgh Post-Gazette* in September.

Jogging the pace with old man time
Over the span of many years.
Showing him up with youthful prime,
Enjoying the envy of his tears.
Playing your game like days of yore,
He has some kick, that's why he's sore.

Holding your own among the best,
And that's where you shine to the fan.
Ready to meet the hardest test.
Rare old bird, you surely can.
In days to come you'll fade we know,
So, here's to you, old Coulter Joe.

The Pirates won the pennant over the Chicago Cubs with Joe's hitting alone. He figured in all four runs that enabled Pittsburgh to beat the Cubs and go into first place. Joe was looking forward to wreaking vengeance against his rival, Babe Ruth.

"How did I acquire the ability to hit curve balls?" Joe repeated the question asked to him by the AP reporter before the series began. "It just seems to come natural. It is the timing and the eye. A hook just seems to suit my swing. As far as I can recall, curves always were easy meat for me. In my first year as a regular, I was the only right-handed batter to hit over .300. I made 112 hits, and I know 100 of them were off curve balls."

They played the first game of the World Series at Forbes Field in Pittsburgh. Joe invited his old friend Jim Borland, the sportswriter from the *Franklin News-Herald*, as his guest. Jim sat with Pearl in the stands behind the Pirates dugout. Showers threatened the start of the game but never appeared, and it stayed a warm 70 degrees. Strips of tickets for three games printed with a value of $16.50 were selling for between $30 and $75 by greedy speculators who knew fans wanted a glimpse of Babe Ruth. Jim and Pearl howled along with the rest of the crowd at the antics of the Baseball Clowns, Nick Altrock and Al Schacht, as they performed their boating and swimming stunt before the game.

Joe and the rest of his teammates stood at attention with their caps over their hearts as the brass band played the *Star-Spangled Banner*. The playing of the National Anthem always gave Joe goosebumps, and this time was no different. He squinted out into the crowd to see if he could find where Pearl and Jim were sitting. He took several deep breaths to try to slow down his racing heart as he heard the umpire yell, "Play ball!"

Babe Ruth made the first Yankee hit, a single, and scored the first New York run. The breaks continued to go against Pittsburgh after that. By the sixth inning, the Yankees were leading 5 to 3. First up was Tony Lazzeri, New York's second baseman and a member of "Murderer's Row." He hit a line drive for a double.

Pirates manager Donie Bush immediately put in Johnny Miljus as his relief pitcher. The curve ball artist prevented any further scoring in the sixth.

In the seventh, Johnny struck out Earl Combs, the Yankees lead-off man. Then Mark Koenig grounded to Joe. Joe tossed him out at first with Johnny covering first base. Joe and Johnny winked at each other. Then Babe Ruth was up to bat. He took a slow ball and singled to center. When Babe Ruth led off first, Johnny picked him off, throwing to Joe, who ran down Ruth after setting up the trap with Glenn Wright at second. That retired the Big Bambino and ended the top of the seventh. Joe raised his glove to the 40,000 fans at Forbes Field as they cheered lustily.

In the bottom of the seventh, Johnny led off for the Pirates and went down swinging.

In the dugout, Joe patted his friend on the back. "That's OK, Johnny. It's not over yet."

In the top of the eighth, Johnny knocked down a Lou Gehrig drive to the mound and threw him out to Joe at first. Miljus then struck out Bob Meusel. Lazzeri hit a grounder to Pie Traynor at third base. Pie then threw the ball almost over Joe's head at first, but Joe caught it and tagged Lazzeri on the baseline.

In the bottom of the eighth, Pittsburgh made three hits. There were two outs when Joe's single drove in shortstop Glenn Wright with the fourth Pirate run to cut the Yankee lead 5 to 4. Joe stood up straight and tall in the dugout after that hit. But Wiley Moore, big and ungainly, hitched up his trousers and tossed one that Earl Smith spanked straight into Lou Gehrig's glove for the final out of the inning.

In the top of the ninth, Dugan and Collins grounded out for New York. Johnny struck out the Yankee relief pitcher for the third out.

In the Pirates last turn at bat, Fred Brickell, who batted for Johnny, ground out. Lloyd Waner's drive to center went right into Combs' hands. Barnhart's drive off Moore's glove was picked up by Lazzeri, who threw to Gehrig at first to end the first game. The Yankees won the first game 5 to 4.

The Yankees had a 6 to 2 win over the Pirates in the second game. The Yankees won the third game 8 to 1 in New York.

Joe and Johnny talked in the dugout after the third game. "We can't let them sweep the series," Joe said. "Do you think God is a Pirates fan?"

"I don't think God is interested in who wins or loses a baseball game. So, I think I should start tomorrow," Johnny said. "I was the only pitcher able to hold them in the first game."

The fourth game on October 8th started in a drizzling mist and with ominous clouds overhead at Yankee Stadium. In the first inning, Combs singled and so did Koenig. Ruth hit a single to right, which scored Combs. Pittsburgh also scored one run in the first inning. The score remained tied 1 to 1 until the fifth inning when Ruth homered, driving in Combs to make it 3 to 1. Pittsburgh came back in the seventh with two runs to tie the score 3 to 3.

Johnny relieved Carmen Hill in the bottom of the seventh when Pittsburgh caught up. Koenig hit an infield single. Ruth hit into a double play—Traynor at third, to Wright at second, to Joe at first. Every time Joe got Ruth out, he pumped his fist to the sky. Gehrig's fly was caught to retire the side.

In the eighth, Pittsburgh had George Grantham at second with two outs and the Yankees decided to walk catcher Johnny Gooch. Miljus was up. Johnny struck out.

Johnny held the Yankees scoreless in the bottom of the eighth. Meusel grounded out. Lazzeri walked. Dugan popped up and out to Joe. Collins singled, advancing Lazzeri to third. Johnny then returned the favor and struck out Yankees pitcher Wiley Moore.

In the top of the ninth, Pittsburgh went down with no score, one, two, three. At the bottom of the ninth, the Pirates took the field and knew their only hope was to hold the Yankees scoreless to go into extra innings.

Johnny seemed to feel the strain. He walked Combs on four balls in a row. Mark Koenig then bunted down the third base line and made it to first. With two men on, Babe Ruth stepped up to bat.

Donie Bush ran out to the mound to talk to Johnny. "Pass up Ruth for Gehrig, and we'll force an out at home plate." Bush said.

"I think I can strike him out," Johnny said.

"Just do what I'm telling you to do," Bush bellowed into Johnny's face as he stood a few inches away from him. Bush made an abrupt 180 degree turn and stomped back to the dugout.

As Johnny threw the first ball to Ruth, Ruth yelled, "Give me a chance!"

At the second and third balls, Ruth yelled, "If I don't do it, Gehrig will!"

At the fourth ball, Ruth screamed, "Oh you, sour son of a bitch!"

Gehrig stepped up to bat. Johnny struck him out with a resplendent curve to the inside edge. Now Johnny only had to dispose of two more from "Murderer's Row": Bob Meusel and Tony Lazzeri. The game could then go into extra innings.

First, he broke a curve ball to the outside corner where Meusel never hits them. The umpire called a strike. A low, outside pitch was a ball. Meusel lunged at a dipping curve and missed. Johnny drove a fast ball shoulder high, but the umpire called it a ball. Meusel fouled one, but then swung again and missed. He was out.

Now Johnny only had to deal with Tony Lazzeri, the Yankees' last hope. He hit a line drive foul to the left off Johnny's first pitch. The next pitch went high and wide. When the catcher, Johnny Gooch, lunged for it, the ball glanced off his mitt and rolled quickly towards the box where Commissioner Landis was sitting. The base runners froze. The crowd hushed as everyone stared at the ball in disbelief. Then Combs came in from third and the game was over.

Johnny hung his head as he headed for the clubhouse.

The next day Joe talked to the press. "This is a blue day for me. This is a blue day for all of us Pirates, but before I start talking about the loss of the game and the World Series, I want to say right here that the Yankees are a great ball club and deserved to win." He continued.

"I'll not get the winning player's end of the purse, but honestly I'm telling the truth that that doesn't worry me nearly as much as the fact that my buddy, my war-time comrade, John Miljus, was the loser along with the rest of us.

"This native Pittsburgher showed more courage in that ninth inning than I have ever seen on any ball field. Just imagine the tight fix he was in with three men on, nobody out, and with almost any kind of batted ball capable of winning the game and the series in that exciting ninth inning.

"Boy, maybe I wasn't pulling for that boy on the mound when he faced Gehrig. I could have hugged him when he struck Lou out. And then when Miljus came through once again to strike out Meusel with those Yankees running and hopping on the base paths and with the crowd in a great uproar, I felt like trying to stop the game to go over and shake him hard.

"Only one more fellow remained to be taken care of, Lazzeri. Then came that awful piece of bad luck which saw Miljus' curve go too high and wide for Johnny Gooch to reach. Combs scored on that pitch and the game and the series passed into history.

"You would know, if you were in the army, what an affection you get for a soldier buddy, and if you realize that Miljus and I were together a great deal in those days across the sea, you'll know just how I felt as I watched John leave the mound to walk slowly off the field and into the clubhouse. Somehow my sympathy for John after his notable work in the ninth surpassed my own regrets that our club passed out of the picture before it managed to hit its best stride.

"If someone had told me that the Yanks or any other ball club could beat the Pirates in four straight games, I'd suspect the man was not altogether sound mentally."

Chapter Eighteen

1928

Pearl shouted, "Surprise!"

Joe took a step back as he opened the door to their darkened apartment. Several of his friends jumped out from behind the sofa, the curtains, and the door to the kitchen and one of them threw on the lights. Although it was the third week in May he was not expecting anything like this.

"You could give a guy a heart attack!" Joe exclaimed. "This is unbelievable." Joe quickly took off his fedora and stored it in their hallway closet. He looked dashing in his tailored suit and wingtip shoes.

Pearl clapped her hands together and laughed. "Happy birthday, darling!"

Soon, jazz music was blaring on the phonograph and everyone was dancing. Pearl served a huge white cake with Happy Birthday, Moon on it. Joe was smiling like a dog at a butcher's window.

"I couldn't fit 37 candles on the cake, so I just did 4," Pearl whispered jokingly in Joe's ear. Pearl looked elegant with her hair in a bob and an azure blue chemise dress.

"It's perfect. I've never been happier," Joe said as he kissed her lightly on the forehead. "I don't believe I could blow out 37 candles, and we wouldn't want to call the fire department."

Joe left Pearl's side to mingle with his other guests. After a few drinks, Steve O'Neill sang a rousing version of "Danny Boy" along with some of the other baseball players. They had their arms around each other's shoulders and were swaying back and forth.

"Everyone, everyone," Joe called out and clinked a knife against his glass to get the partygoers attention. "I want to thank you all for coming out to my birthday party this evening. I was so surprised. But it's also the birthday of my lovely wife Pearl. We both have birthdays in May. She always stays in my shadow, but I want to throw the light on her now."

Steve and the other players then broke into the happy birthday song. First for Pearl and then for Joe. Pearl hid her face in her hands as the group applauded.

Joe's newspaper friend and hunting buddy Jim Borland was at the party. "Hey, Joe, did you hear that some of the owners want to decorate the baseball uniforms with different symbols and insignias?" Jim asked.

"No, I didn't hear that," Joe said.

"Yeah, the St. Louis Browns want to wear a replica of Lindbergh's 'Spirit of St. Louis' on their uniforms. They need Lindy's plane to pull them out of the trenches!" Jim snickered.

"How about a two-foot-long stick of Wrigley's gum across the chest of a Cub's uniform?" Joe laughed along.

"And you know how bad the Phils' stats are? They aren't even in the running? They could embroider Coolidge's 'I do not choose to run' on their shirts," Jim was now laughing so hard he couldn't even take a sip of his beer. Joe bent over, slapping his knee.

Later in the evening after everyone had gone home, Joe and Pearl were cleaning up the apartment. Picking up half-filled glasses and emptying ashtrays, Joe said, "What a great party, Pearl. Thank you."

In June, not long after the big birthday celebration, Joe got some news that he wasn't sure was good or bad. The Pirates traded him and catcher Johnny Gooch to the Brooklyn Robins in exchange for their catcher Charlie Hargreaves. The good news was that Brooklyn insisted on including Joe in the deal, intending to use him at third base. That part made Joe feel wanted. The bad news was that they upset the Pittsburgh fans by kicking out their war hero. And it was bad news for Joe because he had such a short amount of time playing in his hometown. He felt a little like a piece of meat. If anyone wanted to buy him, they could. Joe could understand that the management wanted to trade Johnny after he had missed catching that last pitch in the World Series, but Joe had a great series. Although Joe had devoted his life to baseball, the end comes soon enough. Joe knew he was one of the oldest men in baseball and that he wouldn't be able to keep up with the rigorous demands of the game forever. But he had been hoping he could finish out his career in Pittsburgh.

Joe still handled the bat as if it were a part of himself. He was hitting .402 and began taking a huge black bat to all the games. Although his hitting was great, his old, war-bruised legs just didn't allow him to get around the bases fast enough.

In September, after playing for the Robins for a few months, Joe got some scathing press, and it made him think seriously about retiring from baseball. The Robins played a game against their local rival, the New York Giants at Ebbetts Field in Brooklyn. Ebbets Field was one of the smallest fields that Joe had ever played in. The fans were practically next to him at third base. The crowd was all from the local neighborhood. They either walked there or took the train. The fans in Brooklyn did not like Joe as much as the fans in Pittsburgh had.

The Giants were only ahead by one when Joe stepped up in the ninth inning to pinch hit. The announcer said that Joe walked like a gorilla with his stiff legs creaking at every step. The first pitch was a strike, but Joe did not swing at it. The second pitch was also over the plate. Joe swung at it so violently that he wrenched his left side. Joe staggered backwards and pressed his hands to his side. The crowd booed.

"Are you okay?" the umpire asked him.

His avuncular manager, Robbie Robinson, was ready to send out another hitter to take the third strike. Joe waved him away.

"I'm all right," he said gruffly.

The next pitch was over Joe's head. But the pitch after that, he slammed past the pitcher for a clean hit. In that hit, Joe strained his right side, and he could barely stagger down to first base. The right fielder then grounded out to end the game. The Giants had defeated the Robins 1 to 0. The paper printed all the announcer's comments about Joe walking like a gorilla. There was even a cartoon with a gorilla, dressed in Brooklyn's trademark checkered uniform with the "B" on the chest, knuckles dragging, hopping around the bases. If there was a bright side, the article noted that Joe Harris would be a great hitter even if they rolled him up to the plate in a wheelchair. But Joe didn't agree. He was feeling overwhelmed by the negative press.

By October the Robins season was over. They had won one more game than they lost, but it was still not a very good season. The Robins players scattered to the winds after the season and Joe didn't feel any camaraderie with them. Joe was looking forward to doing some hunting near his home in Franklin.

Joe had no illusions about himself. "I know I'm about through in the big leagues," he said to Pearl. "I'd like to catch on as a manager of some minor league club if I could."

"I've always said, you're a fighter, Joe Harris," Pearl said. "If you set your mind to it, it will happen."

"You know what I'm going to do? I'm going to set up a barnstormer series to show everyone that I would be a great manager." Joe said.

Joe got in touch with some of his old friends. He got Steve O'Neill to catch. Jack Quinn and dapper Rube Walberg of Philadelphia to pitch. George Uhle of Cleveland to play in right field. Bill Sweeney of Detroit to play second base. Joe Hassler at shortstop, Jimmie Foxx at third, and Bing Miller at center field—all of them of the Athletics. Harry Hellmann of Detroit in left field. Joe called his team the Allstars, and he planned to play against the Homestead Grays, a team in the Colored league in southwestern Pennsylvania. He felt sure that the fans would come out to support a few games like this, and he secured Forbes Field for their games. This series would be a great test of the Grays on the baseball field, and Joe was satisfied that the team he put together would prevail.

Even though Joe had 17 putouts in the series, the Homestead Grays beat the Allstars. Walter Cannady was the hitting star of the Homestead team with 10 hits in 12 times at bat against Joe's team. The press called Cannady the laziest man in baseball but there was nothing lazy about his playing against the Allstars.

Cannady's thumb split open when hit by one of Walberg's pitches, and he played on through the pain. Joe played his last game with the Allstars on October 13th, and the results of the games didn't portray Joe as the best manager.

When he got back to Franklin, Pearl asked him to go to the cinema on Halloween before he left on his hunting trip. He was so down on himself, and she wanted to distract him. Pearl was accustomed to the life of a baseball wife. Not only was there glamour, but also there was the challenge of supporting her husband when he had the worst season of his career. As they walked holding hands, they enjoyed seeing the children dressed up in their clown, witch, and hobo costumes, running from house to house. Houses along the street were decorated with carved jack-o-lanterns and paper skeletons. Once inside the theatre, they laughed and laughed at Steamboat Willie on the screen. It was just the relief that Joe needed after his shaky year at the ballpark.

In December, Joe was given his unconditional release from Brooklyn with the 10-year rule. To play any professional baseball under the reserve system, Joe always signed the one-sided contracts and accepted the owners' terms that all the players were offered. The reserve clause in the contract bound the player to the team for as long as the team, not the player, desired. After playing for ten years in the major leagues, the Robins were not extending his contract and there were no other prospects. It looked like Joe's playing days may be over.

Chapter Nineteen

1929

Joe hollered from the bedroom. "Pearl!"

"What is it?" Pearl came running from the front room where she was watching some school children kicking through piles of leaves as they were getting onto a schoolbus. She could tell from the tone of Joe's voice that something was wrong.

Joe doubled over in pain. He grimaced, covered in sweat. "I can't even stand up, my stomach hurts so bad! The pain is shooting from my stomach right through to my back." He began panting.

"I'm calling an ambulance. Maybe you're having a heart attack," Pearl said.

"No! No ambulance, Pearl. I almost died the last time I rode in an ambulance," Joe wheezed and squeezed his eyes shut.

"I'll call my dad," Pearl said.

Pearl ran to the telephone. Her fingers trembled as she dialed on the rotary dial. "Daddy? It's Pearl. Joe's very sick. Can you come and help me get him to the hospital? Thank you, Daddy."

Pearl's father Billy arrived within fifteen minutes. He and Pearl balanced Joe between them, his arms across their shoulders. His feet plodded as if he was stepping over huge rocks. His chin tilted upwards as they loaded him into the back of Billy's car. Joe's face was very pale, almost a shade of green, from the excruciating pain. He moaned as Pearl held his hand until he was laying sideways across the back seat of the car.

"Let's go, Daddy," she said as she got into the front seat of the car and pulled the door closed.

When they arrived at the hospital in Oil City, Pearl ran inside to the desk. "Can someone help me? I think my husband is having a heart attack."

The nurse at the front desk quickly got two orderlies with a stretcher. They carried Joe from the car into the hospital.

Pearl and Billy went into the crowded waiting room. Pearl found an open, hard-backed, wooden chair to sit on. Her father stood next to her with his hand resting lightly on her shoulder. Beside him was a woman holding crutches and wearing a maroon wool coat that smelled of moth balls. There was one boxy wooden desk at the front of the room where the nurse sat. The walls were painted a light green, but Pearl didn't find that soothing. She held a handkerchief tightly in her hands.

"Daddy, why don't you go on home," Pearl said. "I'll call you just as soon as I know something."

"I don't want to leave you here by yourself," Billy said.

"I'll be fine," Pearl said, masquerading as brave and hoping her father wouldn't notice.

"You always were my independent child," Billy said as he kissed her forehead and left the waiting room.

After listening to the clock tick on the wall for what seemed like several hours, Pearl jumped up as a doctor approached her. "Is my husband having a heart attack?" she asked.

The white-coated doctor took her by the elbow and led her to a quiet part of the hallway. "Mrs. Harris, your husband is not having a heart attack. He has a severe case of pancreatitis. We will have to remove his gallbladder as soon as possible. We'll come and get you when we know something."

A few more hours went by. The nurse at the front of the waiting room called her, "Mrs. Harris?"

"Yes, I'm here," Pearl leapt up from her chair like a mountain goat jumping through the air from one rock to another.

"Mrs. Harris, your husband is out of surgery now. You can see him in the main ward."

Pearl walked cautiously down the hallway until she found the main ward. Dozens of beds lined each wall with a white sheet between each one. A small wooden chair sat at the foot of each bed and a small tray table at the side. Joe was about halfway down. He was still asleep when she got to his bed.

"Hi, beautiful," Joe said when he groggily opened his eyes.

Distraught, Pearl started to cry. "I was so afraid that you weren't going to make it."

"Those Jerrys couldn't take me out, Pearl. I wasn't going to let a gallbladder kill me," Joe said. "Please don't cry."

Soon the doctor joined them, and Pearl dried her eyes with the handkerchief that she nervously fidgeted with in her hands.

"Mr. and Mrs. Harris, Joe has come out of this surgery, but I won't lie to you. This will be a tough recuperation. He will need plenty of bed rest. He shouldn't eat any fatty foods. No nuts. No alcohol. He'll be staying in the hospital for a few more days until he's strong enough to go home," the doctor said.

Pearl went home to their apartment in the Park Hotel that evening. All the newspapers were calling her to ask about Joe's condition. She just told them he was very ill and would need some time to convalesce.

A week later, Pearl went to the hospital with a change of clothes for Joe. She was told she could take him home that day. When she got to the main ward, his bed was empty. She went to the nurse's station to find out where he was. She thought maybe they were giving him a shower and shave before she took him home.

"Mrs. Harris, I'm so sorry. Mr. Harris was rushed back into emergency surgery just a few hours ago," the nurse said. "The doctor will speak to you shortly."

Pearl sat on the hard, wooden chair next to Joe's bed. It wasn't long before she saw the doctor approaching from the door to the ward.

"Mrs. Harris, I'm afraid that your husband began to bleed internally. He has significant scar tissue in his abdomen from the accident he survived during the war. That scar tissue didn't allow his gallbladder incision to close properly. Your husband is in critical condition. You should call any of his family members that would like to see him. At this point we've done everything we can for him. I'm sorry."

Pearl couldn't believe what she was hearing. It was just a simple gallbladder surgery. How could this be happening?

Back at her apartment, Pearl first called her father, and then she began contacting Joe's brothers. Although Joe had installed a telephone in their apartment, his family in Pittsburgh couldn't afford a telephone. She sent a Western Union telegram to his closest brother, Jack. Joe had helped Jack buy a farm outside of Pittsburgh when he sold his billiard parlour and bowling alley.

JACK,

REGRET TO INFORM YOU THAT YOUR BROTHER, JOSEPH, IS CRITICALLY ILL IN HOSPITAL AND MAY NOT MAKE IT. PLEASE INFORM THE REST OF THE FAMILY. COME IF YOU ARE ABLE.

PEARL

When Pearl returned to the hospital the next day, Joe was back in his bed. This time, however, he couldn't even lift his head. He was so weak. He laid with his eyes closed.

"Joe," Pearl whispered into his ear. "I know you're strong. You're a fighter. And you will get better. This can't be the end."

A few days later, Jack and David arrived at the hospital. By that time Joe could sit up for short periods of time. Pearl was by his side, holding his hand.

"It's so good to see you," Jack said. "William wanted to come, but someone had to stay back at the farm and take care of the animals."

Joe smiled faintly. "That sounds like William. How is everyone at home?" Joe croaked.

"They're all rooting for you to get better," Jack said.

"Speaking of rooting for me to get better, look at this telegram I got," Joe said to Jack. It took all of his strength to lift the piece of paper from the top of a stack of envelopes on his side table. He grasped the yellow paper between two fingertips and shakily handed it to his brother. He fell back on to his pillow as Jack read out loud.

MOON,

WISHING YOU STRENGTH AND A SPEEDY RECOVERY SO WE MAY FACE EACH OTHER AGAIN.

GEORGE H RUTH

"When I went into my first surgery the Yankees were way behind in the pennant race. Did they make it to the World Series? Did they win?" Joe weakly asked. Pearl shook her head in disbelief that he would even ask such a question in his state. Jack had never seen his brother so frail.

"Always thinking about baseball. That's the least of your worries right now, brother. You need to concentrate on getting better," Jack replied. "But your new friend George and the Yankees didn't make it to the Series. The A's won it."

Joe seemed satisfied with that news and closed his eyes to rest. His brothers tiptoed away from his bed so they wouldn't wake him. Pearl continued to sit by his side holding his hand.

Joe stayed at the hospital for two more weeks. He could sit up for short spells but not much more than that. The nurse would prop an extra pillow under his head.

The Oil City hospital got a daily copy of the *Pittsburgh Press*. On October 29th, the headline read:

HUGE LOSSES IN WALL STREET:

SALES SET ALL TIME RECORD

Pearl read some of the news to Joe, but she didn't want to upset him. They didn't have any money invested in the stock market, but the predictions were that the whole country's economy would suffer. People wouldn't be able to go to baseball games if they had no jobs. On top of the country's bad news, the doctor had been to Joe's bed in the ward that morning and suggested he have another surgery to remove more internal scar tissue.

"Mr. and Mrs. Harris, this scar tissue will cause problems in the future by blocking your intestines. When you're strong enough, we'd like to get some of that scar tissue out of there. In the meantime, we want Joe to have some heliotherapy treatment. We want to put him outside in the fresh air and sunlight to improve his condition," the doctor told Pearl.

A nurse began pushing Joe in a wheelchair out into the hospital courtyard when the weather was relatively warm. There were always a few fair days in the fall in northwestern Pennsylvania. He got a little stronger each day.

One sunny morning he was sitting outside in his robe with his lap covered in a light cotton blanket. Pearl sat beside him on a chaise lounge wearing her sunglasses.

She said, "Oh, honey, I need your help with this clue." Crossword puzzles were the latest craze, and Pearl did the daily one in the *Pittsburgh Press*.

"55 horizontal, 4 letters. Third letter is an 'O.' The clue is: First player to hit homerun in first World Series at bat," Pearl continued as she raised a brow above her sunglasses' frame.

"Let me see that," Joe said as he plucked the folded paper from her hands. The corners of his mouth turned up when he looked back in Pearl's direction.

"M-O-O-N," Joe spelled out loud.

After the third surgery, Joe felt a little better, but his stomach continued to bother him. He got two more surgeries before the doctors felt that all the scar tissue was removed and there would be no bowel blockages. Before all this had happened, Joe thought he wanted to retire but now all he wanted to do was to return to baseball.

Chapter Twenty

1930

It was February, and Joe had only been home from the hospital for a few months.

"Canada?" Joe asked. Joe and Pearl were entertaining Steve O'Neill. His old friend now managed the Toronto Maple Leafs, a minor league team affiliated with the Detroit Tigers. Steve came to Franklin to pay them a visit as Joe was convalescing.

"Sure, and we'd like yourself to come and play for the Toronto Maple Leafs now that you've recovered from your surgery. First you would be goin' to the training camp at Tarpon Springs, Florida, but after you could come and join myself up north," Steve said.

"Well, Florida would be a warm place for recovery from my surgery," Joe chuckled. "In November, the doctors were telling Pearl that I wasn't going to make it. But now they tell me I have recovered from my five surgeries. I thought I was finished with baseball, but now when they tell me I shouldn't play anymore, it makes me more determined."

"No worries," Steve said.

"I'm looking forward to a successful season with you," Joe said. "I accept your offer."

"I don't know as I'll be able to pay you as much as you made in the big leagues, but I think you'd sure like Toronto, me lad," Steve said in his Irish brogue. "It'll bring memories of Pittsburgh, so it will." Steve shook Joe's hand to seal the deal.

With the gallbladder surgeries, Joe lost the 25 pounds of extra weight he had been carrying, although he would have preferred a different weight loss method. Joe had maintained his baseball playing weight since his return from the hospital, following a strict diet so that his pancreatitis wouldn't flare up again. He tried to keep up with his conditioning and got plenty of rest. It would be another year before he turned 40.

In May, Joe stepped onto the field again for the home opener in Toronto. He relished turning his face to the sun and digging his cleats into the dirt. Joe inhaled the smells of grass, popcorn, and cigar smoke all around him. The team played at Maple Leaf Stadium at the corner of Bathurst Street and Lake Shore Boulevard, right on the shores of Lake Ontario. There were only 15,000 fans. Joe thought there would be more considering it was a beautiful spring day with fresh breezes blowing off the lake. But after the stock market crash, attendance at baseball games was down. The Leafs won 6 to 5 over Reading to the delight of the fans who came to the ballpark. Joe played a small part in the opening win, with a two-base hit and a double play when he was at first base.

In June, Joe homered into the left center field stands with two on to give the Leafs a 9 to 8 triumph over the Newark Bears. It was one of the longest hits ever made at the park. Joe tried to get excited about his accomplishments and the team's wins, but the shrinking crowds at the ballparks robbed him of his enthusiasm. He missed the huge crowds chanting, "Moon! Moon! Moon!" when he hit one of those long home runs.

In August, Joe and the rest of the players heard a loud droning sound as they were practicing. Joe looked up from his spot at first base to see the giant airship, the dirigible R100, coming across the Toronto Islands and circling the city. Joe had seen nothing like it. Joe called for his friend Steve to come out of the dugout. He and Steve ran up into the top levels of the grandstands to get a closer look.

"Would you look at that!" Joe said. Joe gasped as the giant airship dipped its nose towards the water of the lake and it looked like the ship was going to crash. But he and the other players cheered as the ship righted itself.

"There we go now," Steve said. "I've never seen anythin' like that."

Joe thought what he had seen was worthy of making a long-distance telephone call to Pearl. "Pearl, you wouldn't have believed it. This giant aluminum, bug-shaped balloon flying in and out of the buildings. It was as long as the baseball stadium," Joe said into the black handset of the phone.

"That's amazing," Pearl said as the telephone line crackled. "I did read about it in the newspapers. It was the first time an airship ever flew across the Atlantic."

"Pearl, I miss you so much," Joe said. "Why don't you come up here for a visit. The stadium is close to the lake. It's so pretty here."

"I'd like that, darling," Pearl said.

Pearl boarded the train for her visit at the end of August. She and Joe stayed at the newly opened luxurious Royal York Hotel in downtown Toronto for one night only because they couldn't afford more than that. It had ten elevators and over a thousand rooms. They had a shower, a bath, and their own radio in their room. They marveled at the large bouquets of fragrant red roses in the lobby as they passed them.

When she entered the room, Joe held open the door, bowed at the waist and swept his hand toward the bed. "Enter, my queen," he said to Pearl. He wanted Pearl to feel special on this trip.

"This room is beyond my dreams," Pearl said. "I've never seen a place so magnificent."

They rode the streetcar around the city and took a picnic with them to have on the beach near the ballpark. Pearl had packed bread, fried chicken and iced tea. The ramparts of Fort York shaded them as they spread out their blanket on the grass near the sandy shoreline of the lake.

Supine on the blanket with his hands behind his head, Joe said, "I want to ask you something, Pearl. Have you ever missed having children? I know we tried and failed."

"Because I never had a child, I don't know if I missed having one. Some people think that life is incomplete without children. But I've been very satisfied with our lives. You've always been enough for me," Pearl said. "How about you?"

"I guess I was heartbroken at the beginning. I suppose I would have liked to have a little boy to throw the ball around with. But now, I think I'm relieved. Ours would have been a difficult life for a child," Joe said pensively.

"You would have made a great father," Pearl said as she tucked her shoulder into the nook of his arm and laid her head on his chest.

After the picnic, they walked to the beach and spread their blanket out on the sand. They changed into their bathing suits in the changing house and dipped their toes in the cool water of

Lake Ontario. The seagulls seemed to be laughing at each other overhead with their sounds of ha, ha, ha. Joe and Pearl watched them chase each other across the sky. When they finished swimming, Joe draped a towel over Pearl's shoulders as she leaned against him. They looked away from the lake and back towards Toronto's skyline. Toronto, with no steel mills, was a much cleaner city than Pittsburgh.

At the end of the day, Joe and Pearl returned to their hotel room, and both fell into the down-covered bed. Joe hugged Pearl close to him and said, "I love you so much. I have another surprise in store for you. But right now, we're going to enjoy this great hotel."

"I love you, too. As long as I'm with you, Joe, it doesn't really matter where we stay. I would be happy in a tent," Pearl said.

"Well, here's the surprise, my darling. I know our ten-year wedding anniversary isn't until next year, but let's celebrate it on this trip. In four hours on the train we can be in Niagara Falls. I know you wanted to go there on our honeymoon," Joe said.

"Oh, Joe, that would be wonderful," Pearl said.

Joe and Pearl took the train to the Canadian side, Horseshoe Falls. The Clifton Hill Hotel looked like a cottage from a fairy tale with a path edged in river rocks and an arched doorway to their room. They hired a car at the hotel to drive them to the falls. From the back seat of the car, they could see the small, white Niagara Falls sign with an arrow pointing to the left. The driver let them out of the car at Queen Victoria Park, and they breathed in the slightly fishy smell in the air. They could hear the water rushing over the falls almost as loud as thunder as they walked through the beautifully landscaped park to the paved overlook. Joe put his arm around Pearl as they leaned over the iron railing. The mist rose like clouds over the river below the falls.

There was a creaky, wooden aerial lift suspended from a wire cable that traveled back and forth across the river on huge wheels above the rapids. Joe and Pearl saw it traversing back and forth from the overlook.

"Would you like to ride on the Spanish Aero Car?" Joe asked Pearl.

"Oh yes, let's do it," Pearl said, despite being frightened about being suspended above the churning water. She knew this was the kind of exciting activity that Joe thrived on. Joe held her trembling hand as they climbed aboard. Fast flowing water crashed over the rapids into a whirlpool below them. They got so close to the falls that they were both soaked from the mist. They couldn't hear each other talk over the water dashing over the falls.

They walked back across the river on the Honeymoon Bridge. Pearl sheltered her eyes with her hand to her forehead and saw a rainbow behind Joe's head in the mist of the falls. When she glanced down, she saw a shiny Canadian penny on the bridge. She picked it up for good luck.

When they got back to the hotel for the evening, Joe reached for a small book of black and white souvenir photos near Pearl's purse that she had picked up in the gift shop. He flipped through the book gazing at each picture. Pearl looked over his shoulder as she hugged him from behind. "This has been a dream come true. I never want to forget this week with you," she whispered in his ear.

Joe returned to his teammates in Toronto and continued his impressive season. He played in 130 games and was batting .335. He led the team in hitting and in runs batted in. His play was so imposing that Steve asked him to manage a short barnstorming trip with Toronto against Montreal. Toronto took 5 of the 7 games. When the barnstorming trip was over, Joe headed back to Franklin.

"You don't know how happy I am to be back in Franklin," Joe said to Pearl.

"You've been gone for seven months. That's the longest you've ever been away," Pearl said. "And after that long hospital stay, I didn't know if your health would hold. I was so happy that I was able to come and visit you at least once, for that wonderful vacation."

"It was just too hard to travel back and forth to Canada to come home between games. Even though I'm slugging the balls, Pearl, I have to tell you, it's hard on me. I'm one of the oldest guys playing now." Joe said.

"Maybe we should think about you retiring," Pearl said. "You invested in your brother's farm when we sold the billiard parlour. We could move to the farm."

That winter Joe got a call from his older brother, Jack. Joe believed in coincidences, and here was another one. Just as he was thinking about retiring from baseball, his brother called with this proposition.

"Joe, why don't you move here to the farm in Plum and help me run it?" Jack asked. "I'm good with the business side of things like transporting the fruit to market in Pittsburgh. But I need help with the day-to-day operations. There are three farmhouses here. You and Pearl could have the stone farmhouse next to the road all for yourselves. You know that's why you invested in the farm in the first place—to have a place to retire to."

"Pearl and I were just talking about that when I got back from Canada," Joe said to his brother. "I'm tired of playing ball. This old body feels used up, Jack."

Chapter Twenty-One

1931

In April Joe headed to spring training camp just as he'd done so many years before. He and Pearl decided to retire to farm life with his brothers, but he needed to tie up a few loose ends first. He still had a contract to finish out the season with the Toronto Maple Leafs.

His manager, Steve O'Neill, had promoted him to assistant coach and pinch hitter. In spite of his health issues, Joe was still hitting over .300.

Throughout the summer, Joe played in 22 games and was at bat 76 times for the Leafs. Joe felt at home at first base and was playing errorless ball. On offense, he was a mountain of strength. But it was a grind.

In August, he and Johnny Miljus were invited as guests at a game between the Pittsburgh Pirates and the Cincinnati Reds for a reunion of the 320th Infantry Trench Mortar Battery of the 80th Division. They held the tribute game, the last of the series, on one of the hottest days of the year. Joe and Johnny stood on the first base line to be introduced to the crowd before the game.

"Johnny, I don't feel well. I'm getting hotter and hotter and I feel a little bit dizzy," Joe said as he waved his ball cap back and forth above his head. The crowd applauded for their hometown heroes.

"Lean up against me," Johnny whispered to his old friend. Johnny held onto Joe's elbow with one hand while he waved his other hand to the fans.

Joe hoped the fans didn't see that Johnny was propping him up. When the introductions were over, they made their way to the dugout. Joe could no longer hear the crowd. He passed out onto the bench.

When he woke up, Joe saw Johnny's face inches from his. Johnny was holding a cup of water to Joe's lips and encouraging him to take a sip. "What happened?" Joe asked.

"You fainted, old man," Johnny said. "I think you are dehydrated. Drink some more."

By the end of the game, Joe had recovered. Pittsburgh won 4 to 3. Joe and Johnny walked through the grandstand, signing baseballs, baseball cards, and programs. Johnny kept a close eye on his friend as they moved through the crowd.

Throughout the end of the summer Joe's health continued to suffer and his shoulder bothered him more than anything else. He was discussing how it felt with his old friend Jim Borland, the sportswriter for the *Franklin News-Herald*.

"Jim, it feels like needles poking me," Joe said. "Listen to this cracking." Joe rotated his shoulder and it sounded like popcorn popping.

"Joe, come with me and meet this doctor friend of mine, Guy Greene. He just lives in Linesville, about forty miles from here. Right on Pymatuning Reservoir," Jim said.

"I've heard about him, Jim," Joe said. "But he's not even a real doctor. Doesn't even have a diploma. He's a bone doctor.'"

"He's a chiropractor," Jim said. "And a lot of the players go to him. Especially from the Pirates. It's very hard to get an appointment with him. But for you, I'll take you to his farm and make the introductions for you."

"If you think it will help, I'll go. What have I got to lose?" Joe said reluctantly.

Jim and Joe drove to The Pines, Greene's summer home. It was a beautiful drive past the Reservoir. The Pines was a tranquil place to recuperate from bone injuries. It had a concrete pool shaded by pine trees, with a statue of a small boy fishing next to the center fountain. Water lilies covered the pond, and there was a colony of cattails in the corner. A dozen large goldfish moved at a slow pace, glinting in the sun just below the water. There was a park bench under the trees where patients could sit and enjoy nature.

At the main entrance to the large barn, which Greene had remodeled to be his clinic, there was a display of rambling roses on a trellis. On the right side of the entrance, there was a rose garden with landscaped walks and a crystal gazing ball on a pedestal in the center. Joe could smell the roses when they walked past.

"Joe, I want to introduce you to Guy Greene," Jim said. Guy Greene had dark hair swept up over his furrowed forehead. Although Guy was Joe's age, his goatee was already salt-and-peppered gray. He was wearing a white doctor's lab coat.

"Pleased to meet you," Joe said to Guy as he shook his hand. Even the handshake caused Joe to wince in pain.

"Your body is a machine," Guy said to Joe. "I can use spinal manipulation to get rid of that pain in your shoulder. Once I have your spine adjusted, it's like lifting your foot off a water hose. The nerves are not cramped any more. Come into my studio."

Joe laid face down on a low padded table. Guy put one hand on his back and steadied that hand by holding the wrist with his other hand. He pushed down hard. Joe heard a pop. He did this several more times along Joe's spine.

After Guy adjusted Joe's back, his shoulder felt much better. "Why don't you both stay for dinner and overnight since you drove so far? You can head back to Franklin in the morning. I would love to hear some baseball gossip. And if you feel like you need another adjustment in the morning, I can do that." Guy said.

Guy's wife Lois served a bountiful spread of food to them, considering it was the midst of the Depression. Lois had the table set with a lace tablecloth, and she arranged some of the roses from the garden into a stunning centerpiece. She set out some deviled eggs for appetizer.

"I hope you like fish," Lois said. "Guy caught these bluegill in the reservoir, and I made them into a loaf with mashed potatoes. Watch for little bones! And I thought I'd serve that with this tomato aspic in a ring with vegetables in the center. All the vegetables came from our garden."

"It all looks delicious," Jim said as Lois poured some lemonade to go along with the meal.

"So, tell us all about what's going on with the Moon Harris," Guy said.

"Not much to tell," Joe said. "I'm finishing up my season with the Toronto team and then I'll be retiring. I'm working with my old friend, Steve O'Neill, in Canada. He's a great guy. He says this will be his last year in Canada. He wants to get back to the States. He's looking to take a management job with

Toledo. The Mud Hens. He wanted me to take over for him in Toronto, but I feel in my bones I'm ready to retire."

"I could feel in your bones that you are ready to retire," Guy joked.

After dinner, Lois showed Joe to his room. Joe loved listening to the bobwhites in the evening. They sounded like they were chirping their names, *Bob White. Bob White.*

He slept with the windows and doors open. There was a delightful breeze, even though there had been sweltering heat in the city. Joe realized he needed the tranquility of a farm.

He felt much better after the adjustment, and in the middle of September, he traveled to Montreal to play a game against the Montreal Royals. Both teams were middle of the pack, so it didn't affect either teams' standings in the International League. This last game between the two teams happened to be a Ladies Day game. The league promoted Ladies Day to get whole families to come to games during the Depression. The Royals picked their most handsome player to put on the posters to entice women.

Joe entered the dugout where he saw Steve cornered by the pitcher. "Man, Steve," the pitcher said. "I'd rather play a double header tomorrow than play on Ladies Day. Their constant cheering. I never know if I struck out the batter or gave up a home run!"

"You'll be fine out there, for sure," Steve said.

"Their shrill voices," the pitcher continued, shaking his head.

"No worries. Just go out and play your game."

"And what can I be doin' for you?" Steve snapped as he turned to Joe.

"What's the matter with you?" Joe asked. "I thought I was acting like a sick hen, but you're always in some corner hiding away from everybody else."

"Aye, I'm homesick, so I am," Steve said. "I'll just be wantin' to return to Scranton and see my family."

"Just get through the end of the season, my friend," Joe said.

After that game, Joe returned to Franklin from Toronto and had to have complete bedrest for two weeks. He was overcome by the intense heat of the summer. The heat combined with how weak he was from his two years of stomach troubles left him little choice but to sit out the rest of the season.

When he got off bedrest, Joe was ready to move to the farm and join his brothers. But he had to admit that he felt useless. Because he was sick at the end of the season, there was no dinner, party, or any other kind of celebration for his retirement. He didn't have a big last game where his retirement was announced. Most of his friends were still playing baseball, and for Joe every day was Sunday now. He had nowhere to go and nowhere to be. He had devoted his whole life to playing baseball. Now that he didn't play anymore, he felt saddened.

"Did I make the right decision? Retiring?" Joe asked Pearl.

"Oh, honey, of course you did," Pearl replied emphatically.

By Thanksgiving Day, most of the Harris clan was at the farm. They had invited their preacher to join them, too. Joe's sisters, Mary and Margaret, had stuffed a large turkey. Joe, Jack, and William got up early that morning, and, since it had snowed lightly, they decided to go rabbit hunting before dinner. The snow was just enough to show the rabbit's tracks. Joe no longer had baseball, but at least he still had hunting. He had to admit that hunting made him a happy man.

Margaret, ten years older than Joe, said, "You boys be back by 3 for dinner, you hear?" Joe thought she sounded just like their mother.

As Joe crossed the back porch to join his brother William, he could smell the pumpkin pies cooling in the pie safe. Mary was in the kitchen whipping up some heavy cream from one of their cows to go on the pies. He could hear the whisk beating against the side of the crock. Mary had enlisted Thomas to help peel the huge sack of homegrown potatoes for mashed potatoes. As soon as he finished that, she sent him to retrieve the preserved vegetables from the cellar.

Pearl was in charge of setting the table. They had to push two large tables together so everyone would fit around. She smoothed the wrinkles out of the best white tablecloths. She carved a large pumpkin in the shape of a basket and then filled it with apples and grapes from the orchard to make a cornucopia.

As the oldest sibling, Enoch carved the turkey.

Although they were in the midst of the worst depression the world ever witnessed, they had a lot to be thankful for. The farm was getting their family through the worst of it. They held hands and said a prayer.

Although Joe thought President Hoover was making a mess of getting the country out of the Depression, the family still listened to him give a Thanksgiving address on the radio after dinner.

The president said, "Our country has cause for gratitude to the Almighty. We have been widely blessed with abundant harvests. We have been spared from pestilence and calamities. Our institutions have served the people. Knowledge has multiplied, and our lives are enriched with its application. Education has advanced, the health of our people has increased. We have dwelt in peace with all men. The measure of passing adversity which has come upon us should deepen the spiritual life of the people, quicken their sympathies and spirit of sacrifice for others, and strengthen their courage."

After dinner, Jack, William, Thomas, and Margaret gathered around the table to sing some hymns. "We gather together to ask the Lord's blessing. He chastens and hastens his will to make known," they brightened the farmhouse with their sweet voices. Joe sat back in his chair and put his arm around Pearl. He could barely wait to join his family in this peaceful place.

Chapter Twenty-Two

1932

On a sunny summer day, Joe walked out onto the porch of the stone farmhouse and looked over his seventy-acre orchard. He thrived on the outdoor farm life. There were 2,000 young apple, peach, and plum trees. The peaches were more established than the other fruit trees, and they were yielding 300 bushels per year. There were seven acres of Golden Delicious apples. The grape crop also yielded 300 bushels.

Joe and Pearl were up an hour before the sun. Joe's father-in-law Billy Hepner and his nephew Neath Painter helped on the farm. They both had lost their jobs. The quality of the Harris crops was known throughout the Pittsburgh market because Jack had been farming for so long. As luck would have it for all their families, the farm was a paying proposition during the Depression years. Joe was even able to hire some out-of-work local men to help with harvesting in the fall.

Joe's brother Jack looked after the transportation of the produce. With Joe's baseball life over, he managed the production aspect of the farm. There were no days off for any of them.

Joe liked to let the dirt run through his fingers as he was out in the peach orchard. Soil and sunlight were the most important things in any orchard. Each peach tree could have 2,000 to 3,000 buds, but the tree could only hold and grow 600 to 700 peaches. So, Joe and his men went through the orchard and thinned out the peaches when they were the size of cherries. Joe hated throwing those baby peaches on the ground. They would pick the peaches by hand, put them in small boxes, and Jack would take them to the market on the South Side of Pittsburgh each night. Joe kept the trees low so they could pick them three or four times over, and they had peaches for most of the summer.

The apple orchard ripened later in the fall. The apples were picked when their skin turned a golden color. They were able to pick the apples and keep some of them in cold storage so they could have them throughout the winter. Joe's nephew Neath stood on the ladder, and Joe stood on the ground below. Neath might not see from his perspective that an apple was ripe. But from the ground below, Joe could tell that it was the right color. Sometimes Joe held one of those round apples in his hand with two fingers and his thumb just the way he held a baseball.

Joe hired some of the local women and children to help with the grape harvest. He grew Concord grapes because they could be used for juice or as table grapes. The women seemed more careful with his vines than the men.

Pearl stepped out onto their clapboard porch next to Joe. "Next year will be even bigger than this one," Joe said to Pearl as he put his arm around her shoulder. "I'd recommend farm life to any retired baseball player who has the energy and enthusiasm for it."

"We're very lucky to have this farm," Pearl said. "Let's sit outside here on the porch and have our lunch. I made some cornbread and milk soup for us." One side of the porch had a painted red porch swing and the other end had two brown wooden rocking chairs.

Pearl lifted the piece of burlap with which she had covered the bowl so flies wouldn't alight on it. She served each of them a bowl of the cold soup as they rocked on the rocking chairs. There was a light breeze. When they finished their soup, they both had a slightly bruised peach. The pinkish-orange-colored peaches that had a few dents in them weren't quite good enough to sell at the market. Joe chomped into the fresh peach fuzz on the skin and made a loud, slurping noise. The juice ran down his arm.

"There's nothing quite like the taste of a fresh peach on a summer day," Joe said. Pearl agreed.

Joe still liked to travel to Pittsburgh to watch the Buccos play when he had a chance. And he listened to the World Series on the radio. Joe remembered his dad telling him about how the Pirates got their nickname. They had been called the Pittsburgh Alleghenys until they stole second baseman Lou Bierbaurer from the Philadelphia Athletics. The Philadelphia papers all called it "an act of piracy on the high seas." The team embraced the scandal and renamed themselves the Pirates in 1891, the year Joe was born. Buccos was short for buccaneers, another name for pirates. The Buccos were destined to be Joe's favorite team.

One morning Joe walked out to the red barn. Barn chores included feeding and watering their two draft horses. The horses were huffing and snorting as they waited for their buckets of grain. After they ate, Joe put them out in the pasture and he mucked out their stalls. Pearl fed the five dozen chickens they had and collected their eggs. She went back to the farmhouse to wash the eggs to sell.

After the chores, Joe lifted the latch on one stall door and sat down on the dirt floor. Six black and white pointer puppies tumbled over his legs. He held up one of the puppies and hugged it close to his face. The puppy gnawed on the end of Joe's nose with its tiny pin-like teeth.

"Can't beat the smell of fresh puppy breath," he whispered to himself.

When Joe stepped out of the barn, he saw a skeletal, tow-headed teenager walking down the dirt road toward him from the farmhouse. The boy limped slightly as he passed the row of pink peonies Joe had planted for Pearl.

"Mr. Harris?" the young man asked timidly.

"Yes, that's me," Joe said. Joe had never seen him before. It wasn't unusual for men to come by the farm looking for work or a hot meal. Pearl left a wooden box by the mailbox with left-over food in it. Sometimes a loaf of bread, some cheese or some damaged fruit from the farm that they were unable to sell. This youth was thin and pale wearing a white T-shirt and jeans. Joe figured him to be about 17 or 18 years old.

The young man cleared his throat. "Sir, you don't know me because we never officially met. But my name is Jasper Reed. I drove here from Beaver Falls. In 1925 you sent me an auto-graphed baseball from the Washington Senators World Series," Jasper said. "I've always been your biggest fan. And I was sick in the hospital that year. I could only listen to the games on the radio, but I got so excited when I would hear the announcers say that you got a hit or made a catch at first base."

Joe smiled. "You don't say! You drove all this way?"

"I wanted to meet the great Moon in person." Jasper said. Joe shook Jasper's hand. Joe could feel every bone protrude in the young man's hand. He still seemed sickly to Joe. "I read in the papers that you had a farm now and it was close enough to Beaver Falls that I could drive here. I also heard that you raise pointer puppies along with all the fruit that you sell now."

"That's right, I do," Joe replied. "You know, a pointer won Best in Show at Westminster this year. Westminster is the big dog show in New York, although I don't care so much about showing dogs. Pointers are handsome dogs, strong and independent, and I breed them for hunting. When one freezes in the field with that front paw up in the air, that's something to see. With its tail pointed to the sky. I've always loved the breed."

"I didn't know all that about them," Jasper said.

"I have a new litter right now in the barn. They are the cutest little critters when they're pups," Joe said.

"Do you think I could buy one from you?" Jasper asked as he looked up into the face of his hero. "We don't have a lot of money, but my parents said I could have one. To remind me of you."

"I tell you what, Jasper. You pick out any one pup and it's yours. Come and have a look," Joe said.

Jasper and Joe went back into the barn where the puppies were. The puppies were making yipping sounds when they heard Joe return. Jasper sat down on the floor. All the puppies came to him except one that held back a little. Dust floating through a ray of sunlight fell on that puppy.

"That guy's a little shy. But I have to tell you, he has the same heart marking on his side that my first pointer had many years ago," Joe said as he remembered his old dog, Jeff.

"That's the one I want," Jasper said.

"Okay! Pick him up and come on into the house and meet my wife, Pearl." Joe said.

Joe and Jasper walked up the dirt road to the stone farmhouse. They went inside and Jasper noticed the black bat and the 1924 Louisville slugger mounted to a wooden plaque above the stone fireplace. There was a curio cabinet in the corner with several signed baseballs and Joe's mitt. Jasper held the squirming puppy close to his chest as he leaned a little closer to look at the two league championship gold rings glimmering in their black jewelry boxes, one from the 1925 American League championship and one from the 1927 National League. He also examined the special ring that the Franklin fans made for Joe after the 1925 World Series.

Joe pulled up the strap of his overalls as he limped into the kitchen. He yelled for Pearl. "Pearl, come and see who this is! Pearl, this is Jasper Reed. He's that young boy we sent the baseball to after the World Series with Washington."

"Come into the kitchen and have some iced tea." Pearl said. "And I see you've been out meeting the puppies." The farmhouse kitchen was cool and inviting in the summer heat, with floral drapes on the windows and a matching floral tablecloth. Pearl opened the wooden icebox to pull out a pitcher of iced tea.

"Mr. Harris said I could take this one home with me," Jasper said excitedly.

Joe and Jasper spent the afternoon talking about baseball. Joe recounted all the famous games and not-so-famous ones. The puppy fell asleep in Jasper's arms.

"You've lived an incredible life, sir," Jasper said as he gently shifted the puppy in his arms and prepared to leave.

"Oh, don't call me sir. That makes me sound so old," Joe said.

"May I call you Moon?" Jasper asked.

"Yes, call me the Moon."

Chapter Twenty-Three

1959

Pittsburgh Post-Gazette, 11 December 1959
EX-BUC STAR, JOE HARRIS, DEAD AT 67
"The Moon" Played For, and Against the Pirates

Funeral services will be held tomorrow in Franklin, PA, for Joseph Harris, former major league baseball player who had the unusual distinction of playing against the Pirates in the 1925 World Series and playing for them two years later.

Harris, 67, one of the sluggers of both the American and National Leagues, died yesterday at his Plum Borough home after battling emphysema for several years.

Harris broke into the majors with the Yankees in 1914, when he played in two games, and then didn't return to the diamond until 1917 with Cleveland.

He was out again in 1918 in service during World War I and then he really began to pepper the ball, hitting .375 in 62 games for Cleveland in 1919 and .310 and .335 for the Boston Red Sox in 1922 and 1923. In 1925 he hit .324 to help Washington to the American League pennant and then batted .440 in a losing cause against the Pirates with three homers.

In 1927, he came to the Pirates and hit .326 in 129 games after taking over the first base job from Stuffy McInnis. The Bucs won the flag—their last—but dropped the World Series to the Yankees, 4 to 0.

Harris is survived by his widow Pearl Hepner Harris, sister Mrs. Margaret Drescher of Leechburg, and three brothers, James and Thomas of New Kensington, and Alexander of Brownsville. Services will be held from the Burger Funeral Home in Franklin with burial in Sunset Memorial Cemetery.

Acknowledgements

Thank you to my cousin Bob Harris for doing most of the initial research on this book.

Thank you to Tammy MacDonald for listening to me read my first draft out loud on Marco Polo and for giving me suggestions on changes.

Thank you to Jayda Freibert, Shaila Richmond, and Kirsten Tartano for reading the initial manuscript and being honest about needed revisions.

Thank you to Jennie R. Harris for being so supportive as the best editor ever.

Thank you to Oliver J. Dimalanta for the book cover design that you somehow snatched out of the inside of my head.

Thank you to Sage Adderley-Knox for being a great writing coach through this whole process.

Thank you to my husband Alan Gavalya who left me alone to write. I love you very much.

And finally, thank you to my readers for spending your valuable time reading my words. It's an honor.

ABOUT THE AUTHOR

Joyce A. Miller is the grandniece of Joe "The Moon" Harris, the title character in her debut historical fiction novel. Miller lives in the Church Hill section of Richmond, Virginia, with her husband and a retired racing greyhound. Before she started writing, Miller worked for over 30 years as a mechanical designer at a nuclear physics laboratory. When she is not writing, Miller can be found dog training, drinking wine, eating stinky cheese, painting, practicing yoga, traveling with her French physicist friends, tap dancing, or volunteering with her greyhound adoption group.

Connect with Miller online at www.joyceamiller.com where you can learn more about her.

CPSIA information can be obtained
at www.ICGtesting.com
Printed in the USA
LVHW041954261120
672558LV00016B/555